MYTHS AND FABLES
Skill-Oriented Language Arts Activities

Written by Judith B. Steffens and Judy F. Carr
Illustrated by Beverly Armstrong

The Learning Works

Edited by Sherri M. Butterfield

The purchase of this book entitles the individual teacher to reproduce copies for use in the classroom.

The reproduction of any part for an entire school or school system or for commercial use is strictly prohibited.

No form of this work may be reproduced or transmitted or recorded without written permission from the publisher.

Contents

Contents
(continued)

To the Teacher

Myths and Fables is a skill-oriented, thematic language arts unit with great appeal for adolescents. It contains individual and group reading lessons that are based on Greek myths and fables and are specifically designed to expand vocabulary, to increase understanding of literary terms, and to develop skill in literal and interpretive comprehension.

The skills associated with **vocabulary development** and emphasized in this book include creating analogies, differentiating between connotation and denotation, understanding synonyms, being aware of multiple meanings, recognizing common root words, and knowing how to use a dictionary and a thesaurus.

The **literary terms** covered in this book include antagonist/protagonist, characterization, climax, figurative language, flashback, foreshadowing, mood, plot, setting, symbol, and theme.

Literal comprehension skills include the abilities to compare and contrast characters or events, to distinguish fact from opinion, to locate specific information, to identify supporting details, to recognize the main idea of a passage or story, to understand the author's purpose, to impose order on ideas, and to place events in sequence.

Interpretive comprehension skills include the abilities to identify cause and effect, to make inferences, to draw conclusions, and to recognize point of view.

A section of individual activity sheets accompanies this unit. You may wish to make these sheets more durable by mounting them on tagboard or card stock and/or by laminating them or covering them with clear contact paper. Then you can make the resulting activity cards readily available as a classroom resource. You will find that they are ideal for individual or small-group reinforcement or enrichment.

You may use these activities in the order presented or select specific ones to match your students' diagnosed skill development needs. To aid you in making such selections, each activity has been identified by both skill and title in the table of contents. A boxed explanation or definition with examples is provided for each term or concept introduced. Also provided are a bibliography of related literature that is appropriate for junior and senior high students, a pretest and a posttest for measuring student progress, and an answer key for the tests and for all of the activity questions that are not open-ended.

Myths and Fables may be used as an independent unit with both homogeneous and heterogeneous classes, as an enrichment unit, as a source of individual skill lessons, or as a supplement to any basal text.

How to Use This Book

The skill sheets, group activities, and individual activity sheets included in this book can be used in many ways.

	Day 1	Day 2	Day 3	Day 4	Day 5
Homogeneous Group	Group activity to introduce skill Assign individual reading selection to class to be finished as homework.	Individual skill sheet Review the individual skill sheet. Check understanding and application of the concept, term, or skill.	Vocabulary—either a general lesson or a lesson related to the reading selection Record vocabulary in a notebook. Review and collect skill sheets.	Follow-up skill lesson directly related to the reading selection Review skill lesson with class. Collect, correct, and save skill lesson.	Enrichment Day Independent myth or fable reading or Individual activity sheet or Group activity
Heterogeneous Group	Group activity to introduce skill Assign individual reading selection to class to be finished as homework.	Individual skill lesson for entire class Confer with Group A to discuss the reading selection while Groups B and C complete the skill lesson and begin vocabulary work.	Confer with Group B while Group C completes vocabulary work. Confer with Group C while Groups A and B complete vocabulary work.	Follow-up lesson directly related to the reading selection Use one lesson applicable to the entire reading selection or create separate follow-up lessons for each part.	Enrichment Day Story sharing or Independent myth or fable reading or Individual activity sheet or Group activity
Basal Reader	Use individual skill sheet and group activity ideas to introduce and reinforce skills found in the reading assignments.				
Notes	1. Assign independent reading of myths or fables as part of this unit. 2. Give quizzes as needed to hold student interest and check progress. 3. Use individual activity sheets for optional enrichment or as required assignments. 4. Use the Reading Skills Checklist on page 108 to keep a record of the reading skills students have mastered and those that need additional reinforcement.				

Pretest

Think about a myth that you have read. Use it to answer the questions below.

1. Identify the myth you have in mind by writing its title and/or the names of the most important mythological characters and creatures it is about.

_____

_____

_____

_____

2. From what point of view is the myth told? By whom?

_____

_____

_____

3. Who is the protagonist in the myth? What does he or she represent?

_____

_____

_____

4. If there is an antagonist in the myth, identify him or her. If there is none, describe the challenge the protagonist faces.

_____

_____

_____

5. Briefly describe the setting of the myth.

_____

_____

_____

6. In a single sentence, summarize what happens in the myth.

_____

_____

_____

Pretest
(continued)

7. List in chronological order five major events that occur in the myth.

a. _____

b. _____

c. _____

d. _____

e. _____

8. Write one fact and one opinion about this myth.

Fact: _____

_____

Opinion: _____

_____

9. Most myths provide supernatural explanations for natural events. Tell what natural event is explained in the myth you read and describe the *natural* cause of this event.

_____

_____

_____

_____

10. What is the climax of this myth? At what point in the story does it occur?

_____

_____

_____

_____

11. Describe one way in which the end of the myth is foreshadowed.

_____

_____

_____

12. List three adjectives that describe the mood of the myth.

a. _____

b. _____

c. _____

Pretest
(continued)

13. Compare any two gods or goddesses described in the myth or contrast any mortal with any god or goddess in the myth.

_____

_____

_____

_____

_____

_____

_____

_____

_____

14. When an author writes or tells a story, the primary purpose can be to inform, to persuade, or to entertain. What was the author's purpose in writing or telling this myth?

_____

15. Complete the following analogy.

An <u>odyssey</u> is to a <u>journey</u> as a <u>prophecy</u> is to a
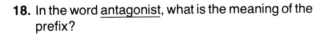_____ .

15. _____

16. Write a synonym for the word <u>panic</u>.

16. _____

17. What is the meaning of the underlined word in the sentence below?

At dawn the <u>detail</u> of men left for Ithaca.

17. _____

_____

18. In the word <u>antagonist</u>, what is the meaning of the prefix?

18. _____

19. In the word <u>justifiable</u>. What is the meaning of the suffix?

19. _____

20. Context clues are familiar words that help the reader determine the meanings of other, unfamiliar words. There are four important kinds of context clues: restatement, example, comparison, and contrast. What kind of context clue to the meaning of the underlined word are you given in the sentence below?

Because he had a headache, he left the <u>pandemonium</u> of one room for the quiet solitude of another.

20. _____

Name _____

Greek Myths

Both children and adults find enjoyment in Greek myths. The appeal of these tales today, long after the civilization that created them has disappeared, is probably the result of an ingenious blending of fantasy, human foibles, and a good story line.

It is generally believed that the early Greek myths, dating from approximately 1500 B.C., were created to explain natural occurrences. Ancient Greeks, frightened by lightning, puzzled by echoes, or awed by the rising sun, developed imaginative stories to explain these phenomena. Through their storytelling, lightning was transformed into bolts hurled in anger by Zeus; echoes, into the moaning of lovesick maidens; and the rising of the sun, into a luminous chariot driven across the sky by the god Helios.

With these tales of gods and goddesses, the Greeks could also account for the vagaries of daily life: if their crops failed, Demeter was unhappy; if their businesses prospered, Athena favored them.

The Greeks used myths not only to explain otherwise puzzling natural phenomena and daily occurrences, but also to teach moral values and to provide a religious framework for their existence. They built temples to honor the gods and goddesses named in their myths. The temple to Apollo at Delphi is well known, and the temple to Athena is perhaps the most celebrated in the world. Called the Parthenon, this temple was built during the administration of Pericles and stands atop the Acropolis in Athens, Greece.

Yet, even as the Greeks worshiped these deities, they imbued them with very human qualities. Like mortals, the Greek gods loved, argued, fought, dallied, sulked, and exulted. To be sure, they lived atop Mount Olympus, drank a sweet nectar called ambrosia, and were immortal; but each god or goddess was also vulnerable, even as the Greeks, themselves, were vulnerable.

Understandably, as the myths were told and retold, they changed. They grew rich in detail. Exploits of the gods became more exaggerated, and heroes battled incredible monsters like minotaurs against seemingly insurmountable odds.

By 800 B.C., when Homer wrote his epic poems, the *Iliad* and the *Odyssey*, myths were viewed by many as entertaining stories rather than as explanations of the unknown. Indeed, by the sixth century B.C., the development of naturalistic explanations by Greek philosophers had changed the role of myths substantially.

It is fortunate that, when the Romans conquered the Greeks, Latinized versions of the Greek myths survived. Even after the advent of Christianity and the destruction of the Roman Empire, Greek and Roman myths continued to be read and enjoyed. And they are still with us today—fascinating tales that tell us much about the people who created them, even as they entertain us with fantasy, humor, and pathos.

Name_____

Align in Time

> **Sequencing** means putting events in chronological order—the order in which they actually occurred.

Read Greek Myths on page 10. Then use a biographical dictionary, an encyclopedia, or a history text to discover the years in which each of these events occurred. First, put the events in sequence by numbering them from 1 through 12. Then, indicate the correct position of each event by letter on the time line.

_____ **a.** Rome is sacked by the Vandals.

_____ **b.** Crete is unified under one or two dynasties.

_____ **c.** Julius Caesar, a Roman general, conquers Gaul, an ancient region of Europe that included most of what is now France and northern Italy.

_____ **d.** Jesus Christ is born; and the Christian religion, which is based on his teachings, has its beginnings.

_____ **e.** The first Greek myths are told.

_____ **f.** Metellus defeats Andriscus, and Macedon becomes a Roman province.

_____ **g.** Alexander the Great rules Greece.

_____ **h.** Homer writes the *Iliad* and the *Odyssey*.

_____ **i.** The Roman Republic is founded.

_____ **j.** The Greek city-states are formed.

_____ **k.** The city of Rome is founded.

_____ **l.** The Cretan civilization spreads to Greece.

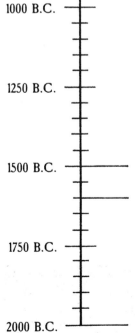

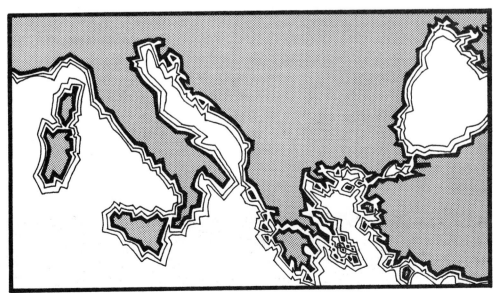

An Olympic Challenge

To **compare** is to show the ways in which similar things are alike or different. To **contrast** is to show the ways in which unlike things are different.

On pages 13 and 14 are two posters advertising the Olympics. One poster is for an ancient competition that might have taken place in Olympia, Greece, in 448 B.C. The other is for the modern competition held in Los Angeles, California, in A.D. 1984. Compare these two posters. On the lines below, record five similarities and five differences between them.

Similarities

1. _____
_____

2. _____
_____

3. _____
_____

4. _____
_____

5. _____
_____

Differences

1. _____
_____

2. _____
_____

3. _____
_____

4. _____
_____

5. _____
_____

JOIN US FOR THE EVENTS
OF THE
LXXXIInd OLYMPIAD

HONOR THE GODS WHILE YOU ENJOY YOURSELF AND WATCH INCOMPARABLE COMPETITION.

SEE OUTSTANDING YOUNG MEN FROM ARGOS, ATHENS, CORINTH, SPARTA, AND OTHER CITY-STATES PARTICIPATE IN ATHLETIC, MUSICAL, AND POETIC EVENTS.

- WITNESS BREATHTAKING RACES OF EVERY CONCEIVABLE TYPE, FROM FOOTRACES TO CHARIOT RACES.

- CHEER AS PERENNIAL FAVORITES LIKE MILO OF CROTON ARE CHALLENGED BY NEWCOMERS IN THE WRESTLING EVENTS.

- MARVEL AT THE SKILL AND ENDURANCE DISPLAYED BY PARTICIPANTS IN THE PENTATHLON, A FIVE-EVENT COMPETITION THAT INCLUDES THE BROAD JUMP, THE DISCUS THROW, FOOTRACING, THE JAVELIN THROW, AND WRESTLING.

- THRILL TO THE LIFE-AND-DEATH STRUGGLE OF THE PANCRATIUM, A HAND-TO-HAND COMBAT THAT ENDS IN DEATH FOR ONE OF THE COMBATANTS.

- APPLAUD AS THE EMPEROR AWARDS THE COVETED OLIVE WREATHS TO THE FORTUNATE WINNERS.

PLAN NOW TO VACATION IN OLYMPIA. CAMP AND PICNIC ON THIS PLAIN IN ELIS. SEE THE GAMES. TOUR THE NEARBY TEMPLES TO ZEUS AND HERA. MAKE YOUR STAY A TIME OF CONTEMPLATION, WORSHIP, AND CELEBRATION.

Join Us for the Events
of the
XXIIIrd OLYMPIAD

See hundreds of outstanding young men and women from as many as 140 countries compete in a variety of sports events.

- Witness competition in a breathtaking array of water sports, including canoeing, diving, rowing, swimming, water polo, and yachting.

- Cheer your track and field favorites as they compete in a total of forty-one walking, running, jumping, and throwing events.

- Marvel at the skill and endurance displayed by participants in the marathon and in the modern pentathlon, the heptathlon, and the decathlon.

- Admire the grace of the gymnasts and the strength of the weight lifters.

- Applaud the members of your favorite basketball, hockey, soccer, and volleyball teams.

**Plan now to
vacation in Los Angeles.
See the games.
Visit nearby tourist attractions.
Take part in Festival,
an Olympic Celebration of the Arts.
Make your stay an experience
in the arts, culture, history, and sports.**

History in the Making

> When you **locate information**, you look in the library card file, in indexes, and elsewhere to find the specific facts and figures you need for a project or report.

First, read this list of projects. Second, select the one you would like to do, and put a check mark in the box beside it. Next, locate the specific information you need for the project, and list the sources of this information in correct bibliographic form on the lines below. Then, get your materials together, and do the project. Finally, share your finished project with the class.

☐ Create the menu for a Greek banquet.

☐ Write a diary entry in which a student in ancient Greece describes an average school day.

☐ Draw a floor plan for a typical house in ancient Greece.

☐ Build a model of an ancient Greek house.

☐ Draw typical outfits for a man, a woman, a young boy, and a young girl in ancient Greece.

☐ Fashion a Greek outfit from cloth.

☐ Build a diorama depicting the recreational opportunities available to the ancient Greeks.

☐ Make a display showing the writing equipment used in ancient Greece.

☐ Create a montage or a mobile representing three or more types of Greek art.

☐ Write a series of classified advertisements for jobs that were common in ancient Greece.

☐ Write a letter from an adult inhabitant of ancient Greece to a younger resident of the modern world describing an ordinary workday or offering timely advice.

☐ From clay, fashion two different kinds of Greek vases.

Sources of Information

_____

_____

_____

_____

_____

Dictionary Devoteze

> Watch enthusiasm and knowledge of the dictionary grow as class lexicographers create a Greek "pictionary."

Materials Needed

index cards
a box, empty coffee can, hat, or other widemouthed container
pencils
lettering pens
crayons or felt-tipped marking pens in a variety of colors
a folder or binder of some sort

Instructions

Before Class

1. Throughout this unit on myths, have class members look for words that have come into the English language from Greek mythology.
2. Make index cards available in the classroom, and encourage students to record each word they find on a separate card.
3. Place these cards in a box, coffee can, hat, or other similar widemouthed container.
4. Continue collecting cards in this fashion until there are enough words so that each member of the class can have one.

During Class

1. Tell students that they are going to create an illustrated dictionary of words that have come into the English language from Greek mythology.
2. Explain that each student is to draw a card from the container and to create a one-page illustrated dictionary entry for the word on the card. The entry is to include the following items: (a) the word, (b) its pronunciation, (c) its part of speech, (d) its definitions, and (e) an illustration of it.
3. Have each student draw a card from the container.
4. Distribute the needed materials, and have students go to work.

Follow-up

Collect the finished pages and display them on a dictionary skill bulletin board, or put them in alphabetical order and bind them for use in your classroom or for donation to the school library.

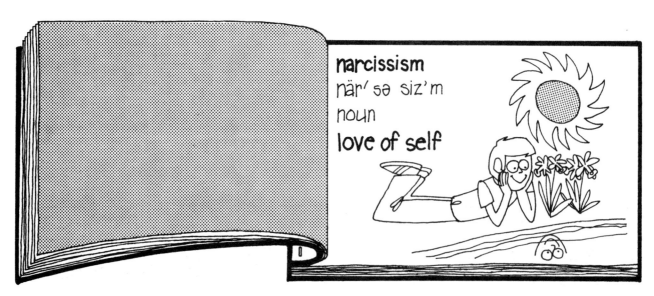

narcissism
när′ sə siz′m
noun
love of self

Outline Odyssey

To write the text for any paragraph, you need a topic, or **main idea**, and you need the details to support that idea. These **supporting details** clarify your meaning or idea and complete the word picture you are trying to create.

As you reread the introduction to Greek mythology on page 10, locate details to support each of the statements written below. Write these details on the numbered lines beneath the statements they support.

A. Greek myths were created to explain natural occurrences.

1. _____
2. _____
3. _____

B. The Greeks used myths to provide a religious framework for their existence.

1. _____
2. _____
3. _____

C. The Greeks attributed human qualities to the deities they worshiped.

1. _____
2. _____
3. _____

D. As the myths were told and retold, the characters and events in them changed.

1. _____
2. _____
3. _____

E. When science supplanted myth as a way of explaining some natural occurrences, these stories continued to be read and enjoyed.

1. _____
2. _____
3. _____

Test your outline. Use it to write your own introduction to mythology. If it is complete and well constructed, you should be able to write your essay without looking back at the one on page 10.

Name_____

The Pantheon—A Family Affair

> **Sequencing** means putting events, facts, or objects in some meaningful order. For events, the order most often used is chronological. Events put in **chronological order** are arranged according to the time at which they occurred.

The English word **pantheon** comes from the Greek word *Pantheon*, the name given by the Greeks to a temple for all of their gods. Today, this word is used to mean "all of the officially recognized gods and goddesses of a people or culture."

The ancient Greeks were eager to understand the natural forces that were at work in the world around them. In some instances, they sought scientific explanations. In other instances, they attributed these natural phenomena to the actions of supernatural beings—gods and goddesses who controlled the rising of the sun, the falling of the rain, the fruitfulness of the earth, and the movements of the waters in the seas.

Each deity in the Greek pantheon had an area of responsiblity. Thus, the Greeks knew which god or goddess to pray to before they fought or hunted, which one to thank when they were victorious in battle, and which one to blame when they suffered economic setbacks or military defeats.

When the Romans conquered Greece, they adopted the Greek pantheon, but they Latinized the names of its members and, in some instances, changed their roles.

Below is a table in which the most important Greek gods and goddesses are listed, their roles are described, and their Roman counterparts are named. Read this table carefully.

Greek Deity	Description or Area of Responsibility	Roman Deity
Gaea	Earth (or Mother Earth)	Tellus
Uranus	Heaven (or Father Heaven); husband of Gaea	
Cronos	son of Uranus and Gaea; youngest of the Titans	Saturn
Rhea	daughter of Uranus and Gaea; wife of Cronos; mother of Demeter, Hades, Hera, Hestia, Poseidon, and Zeus; goddess of the earth	Ops
Zeus	son of Cronos and Rhea; ruler of heaven; god of rain; king of the gods	Jupiter
Hera	daughter of Cronos and Rhea; sister and wife of Zeus; mother of Ares, Hebe, and Hephaestus; goddess of marriage and womanhood; queen of the gods	Juno

The Pantheon—A Family Affair
(continued)

Greek Deity	Description or Area of Responsibility	Roman Deity
Aphrodite	created from the remains of Uranus, which had been thrown into the sea; goddess of love and beauty; patroness of seafarers and of war; most beautiful of all the goddesses; had the power to grant irresistible beauty to mortals	Venus
Athena	sprang forth fully grown and in complete armor from the forehead of Zeus; goddess of truth and wisdom, justice and war; defender of Athens; patroness of the arts and trades	Minerva
Poseidon	son of Cronos and Rhea; husband of Gaea (Mother Earth); originally lord of earthquakes and freshwater streams; later god of the sea and of horses and horse racing	Neptune
Hades	son of Cronos and Rhea; husband of Persephone; king of the lower world; giver of all blessings that come from within the earth, including both crops and precious metals; god of wealth; also called Aides, Aidoneus, Orcus, Tartarus, and Pluto	Dis *or* Dis Pater
Demeter	daughter of Cronos and Rhea; sister of Zeus; mother of Persephone; goddess of the earth's fruits, especially corn	Ceres
Apollo	son of Zeus and Leda; twin brother of Artemis; patron of archery, music, and medicine; protector of law and defender of the social order; closely associated with the sun	
Artemis	daughter of Zeus and Leda; twin sister of Apollo; originally associated with birth and care of the young; later viewed as protector of maidens and goddess of the hunt; often represented by a bear or bow; closely associated with the moon	Diana
Ares	son of Zeus and Hera; handsome but savage god of the warlike spirit	Mars

The Pantheon—A Family Affair
(continued)

Greek Deity	Description or Area of Responsibility	Roman Deity
Hermes	son of Zeus and Maia; herald of Zeus; messenger of the gods; god of eloquence, prudence, and cleverness; inventor of the alphabet, astronomy, gymnastics, weights, measures, and the lyre; god of the roads; protector of travelers	Mercury
Hephaestus	son of Zeus and Hera; god of fire; skilled worker in metals who made armor, weapons, and ornaments for the gods	Vulcan
Hestia	daughter of Cronos and Rhea; sister of Zeus; maiden goddess of the fire burning on the hearth and of domestic life in general	Vesta
Hebe	daughter of Zeus and Hera; goddess of youth; waited upon the gods, filling their cups with nectar; had the power to make old people young again	Juventas

On a separate sheet of paper, draw a family tree on which you put the births of these deities in chronological order and show the familial relationships that existed among them.

```
        Uranus ———— Gaea
       (Heaven)      (Earth)


         Cronos ——— Rhea


Hestia   Demeter   Hades   Poseidon   Hera — Zeus
```

Chaotic Creation

> Watch order replace chaos as your students work together to organize this account of the creation of the world. Statements on the cards contain verbal clues to help them arrange the events in chronological order.

Materials Needed

Chaotic Clue Cards on page 22
scissors
index cards or tagboard
glue or paste

Instructions

Before Class

1. Photocopy page 22.
2. Cut the cards apart along the broken lines.
3. To make these cards more durable, glue them to index cards or tagboard and laminate or cover with clear Contact paper.
4. Arrange for students to sit in a large circle.

During Class

1. Remind class members that **sequencing** means putting events, facts, or objects in some meaningful order. Events are often put in **chronological order**, that is, they are arranged according to the time at which they actually occurred.
2. If there are more than twenty students in the class, play the game with a smaller group or ask students to work in pairs.
3. Distribute one card, face down, to each student or team and caution that these cards are *not* to be turned over until the class is told to begin.
4. Explain to the class that each card describes one event in the creation of the world as the Greeks understood it. Players are to arrange these events in chronological order *without* exchanging cards. All information must be shared orally, and all players must remain seated throughout the entire activity.
5. Once the activity has begun, observe and record the steps the group uses to organize itself and the events, but do not help in any way.
6. When the activity is finished, have the account of creation read aloud as a cohesive whole. Ask each student to read his or her card in the correct sequence.
7. Help students discuss the ways in which they went about organizing themselves and sharing information, and then suggest what they might do differently next time.

Follow-up

After students have had a chance to discuss the Greek view of creation, distribute the skill sheets on pages 18–20. Explain that this time students are to work individually to put the births of gods and goddesses in the Greek pantheon in order and to show the familial relationships that existed among these deities.

Chaotic Clue Cards

A

After the birth of her sixth and last child, Rhea tricked Cronos into swallowing a rock and then hid the child—Zeus—on earth.

B

Zeus and his brothers and sisters went to live on Mount Olympus, where they ruled over the earth.

C

The Greeks believed that the earth was formed before any of the gods appeared.

D

Then Zeus and his brothers waged a mighty battle against Cronos and the other Titans.

E

Finally, Gaea could not bear Uranus's unkindness to the Cyclopes and the Hundred-Handed Ones any longer.

F

Cronos and the Titans were defeated when Zeus ambushed them with the help of the Hundred-Handed Ones, and they panicked and retreated.

G

Thinking it was wine, Cronos drank the mixture and promptly regurgitated his five other children, fully grown.

H

Uranus let the Titans roam free, but he imprisoned the Cyclopes and the Hundred-Handed Ones beneath the earth.

I

Cronos married his sister Rhea, and they had six children.

J

Now Cronos became king of the universe.

K

Cronos and the Titans were imprisoned in the earth, where their fighting still causes earthquakes from time to time.

L

The gods, as the Greeks knew them, all originated with Father Heaven and Mother Earth.

M

Rhea and Zeus connived against Cronos by mixing a noxious drink for him.

N

Gaea joined Cronos, one of the Titans; and together, they overcame Uranus, killed him, and threw his body into the sea.

O

Zeus grew up on earth and was brought back to Mount Olympus as a cupbearer to his unsuspecting father.

P

To protect himself, Cronos swallowed each of his first five children—Hestia, Demeter, Hera, Hades, and Poseidon—immediately after birth.

Q

Father Heaven was known as Uranus, and Mother Earth, as Gaea.

R

Aphrodite, goddess of love and beauty, later rose from the sea where Uranus's body had been thrown.

S

Uranus and Gaea raised many children. Among them were the Cyclopes, the Titans, and the Hecatoncheires, or Hundred-Handed Ones.

T

At the time of Cronos's marriage to Rhea, Gaea prophesied that one of his children would overthrow Cronos, as he had overthrown Uranus.

Name_____

Spin-offs

> **Roots** are the simple words from which longer and more complex words are formed by means of spelling changes or the addition of prefixes or suffixes. Unlike **base words**, which are complete English words (for example, *king*) to which endings may be added to form other words (for example, *kingdom*), root words seldom stand alone in English.

Greek roots form one thread from which the English language has been woven. For example, such words as *telegraph, telephone,* and *television* share the Greek root *tele* and are related in meaning.

How many words can you spin off the word *telephone*? On a separate sheet of paper, draw a spiral in which the lines are at least one-fourth of an inch apart. In the center, write the word *telephone.* Next to it on the spiral, write a word that contains either *tele-* or *-phone.* As you continue to spin, assure silky smooth transitions by buildng each new word on a root from the preceding word. To give you ideas, some common Greek roots are ensnared in a box at the bottom of this page. If you can't find a word with the root you need, simply leave space and begin a new strand by using a word with a different root.

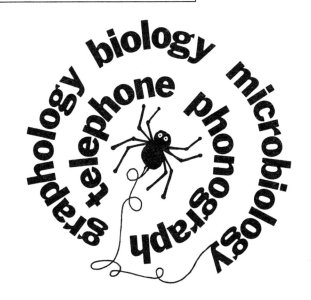

Roots

Greek Word	Meaning	English Form	Meaning
autos	self	*auto-*	self
bios	life	*bio-*	life
chronos	time	*chrono-*	time
demos	the people	*demo-*	people
derma	the skin	*derma-, -derm*	skin
graphos			
from *graphein*	to write	*-graphy*	writing
kratos	rule, power	*-cracy*	rule, power
		-crat	participant in or supporter of
logos	words		
logia	sayings or teachings	*-logy*	science or study of
mikros	small	*micro-*	small
phone	a sound	*phono-, -phone*	sound
photos	a light	*photo-*	light
podos	the foot	*pod*	foot
tele	far off	*tele-*	distant, remote
thermos	hot	*thermo-, -therm*	having to do with heat or temperature

Celestial Symbols

> A **symbol** is an object, person, place, or event that can be used to stand for, represent, or suggest something else because of traditional association, emotional content, or accidental resemblance. For example, an apple may be used to suggest school because of traditional association. For the same reason, a four-leaf clover symbolizes good luck.

Modern advertising is filled with symbols taken from Greek and Roman mythology. On the lines below, identify each symbol. Then briefly describe its mythological association and its modern use.

1. *Symbol:* _____
   Association: _____
   Modern Use: _____

2. *Symbol:* _____
   Association: _____
   Modern Use: _____

3. *Symbol:* _____
   Association: _____
   Modern Use: _____

4. *Symbol:* _____
   Association: _____
   Modern Use: _____

5. *Symbol:* _____
   Association: _____
   Modern Use: _____

Olympian Verse-ality

In this game, students draw conclusions from facts given on twelve rhyme cards to match these cards with the names of twelve gods and goddesses.

Materials Needed

Olympian Verse-ality Cards on page 26
one large piece of poster board
twenty-four book card pockets or other small envelopes
glue or paste
black felt-tipped marking pen
scissors
index cards or tagboard

Instructions

Before Class

1. Glue the pockets to the poster board in four rows of six each.
2. Using a marking pen, number the first twelve pockets from 1 through 12 and letter the second twelve pockets from A through L.
3. Photocopy page 26.
4. Cut the copied Olympian Verse-ality Cards apart along the broken lines.
5. To make these cards more durable, glue them to index cards or tagboard and laminate or cover with clear Contact paper.
6. At random, insert each of the god or goddess cards, face down, in one of the numbered pockets.
7. Likewise at random, insert each of the rhyme cards, face down, in one of the lettered pockets.

During Class

1. Divide the game participants into two equal teams.
2. Remind them that **drawing conclusions** means reaching decisions or making judgments based on a body of evidence or a group of facts.
3. Explain that the names of Greek deities are printed on the cards in the numbered pockets and that rhymed facts about these deities are printed on the cards in the lettered pockets.
4. Tell game participants that, from these facts, they are to draw conclusions that will enable them to match each god or goddess with his or her rhyme.
5. To begin play, ask a member of one team to call a number from 1 through 12 and a letter from A through L.
6. Remove the designated cards from their pockets and turn them face up. Ask the caller to state whether or not the two cards match. If they do and the caller states so correctly, the caller's team gets the cards, one point, and another opportunity to match two cards. If the two cards do not match or the caller says they do not match when they do, play passes to the other team.
7. Play continues in this fashion until all of the cards have been matched and twelve correct pairs have been formed. At this time, the team with the most pairs, or points, wins.

Follow-up

Create other similar concentration games to introduce or reinforce skills taught in this unit.

Olympian Verse- atility Cards

Zeus **1**	Hera **2**	Poseidon **3**
Hades **4**	Athena **5**	Aphrodite **6**
Apollo **7**	Artemis **8**	Hermes **9**
Hestia **10**	Hephaestus **11**	Demeter **12**

F
King of the gods
On Olympus so tall,
His thunderbolt
Causes many to fall.

L
When a message
Olympians send,
On this god
They depend.

E
Though vengeful and jealous,
She is the queen;
Both the cow and the peacock
Know that she's mean.

K
The fire on the hearth
Burns warm and clear
When this home-protecting
Goddess is near.

D
Powerful ruler
Of the foamy deep,
A three-pronged spear
He's known to keep.

J
Known as the smith god
Throughout the land,
By Zeus he was given
Aphrodite's hand.

C
In the lower world, he
Tried to keep Persephone.

I
When her daughter, Persephone,
Was stolen below,
This goddess declared
That nothing would grow.

B
She sprang from her father's
Head, they say;
She's known for her wisdom
To this day.

H
Of music, he's patron;
Of Artemis, he's twin.
He protects social order
And oversees medicine.

A
Love and beauty
Are her domain,
Though her husband
Longs for both in vain.

G
Skillfully she hunts
With her arrow and bow;
That she never married,
We all know.

Arachne

Arachne, a young Greek woman, prided herself on her ability to weave. She spent hours at her loom, creating intricate tapestries filled with marvelous colors. Soon her fame spread, and people from nearby villages and towns flocked to her home to watch her work.

Flattered by the attention she was receiving, Arachne began to boast. "I've spent hours learning my craft," she declared. "Why, no one can match me—not even the goddess Athena, herself." The crowd gasped as she went on, "If we were to compete, I'm sure that I would be declared the winner, for my skills are finer and my technique, more polished."

Soon tales of the young woman's boasting reached the ears of Athena, patroness of the arts, crafts, and skilled trades. Curious about Arachne's skill and angered by her impudence, Athena disguised herself as an elderly woman and traveled to Arachne's home.

The goddess stood for a time among the crowd, watching the young girl work and listening to her boast. Then she spoke. "Foolish girl," she said. "Have you not heard tales about those who have angered the gods? Seek forgiveness from Athena for your presumptuousness now, before it is too late."

"Never," shrieked Arachne. "I owe no mortal or god thanks for my talent. I only wish that Athena were here. Then we'd see who is the better weaver."

At that moment, Athena's disguise fell away, and she stood revealed as the goddess of wisdom and the defender of Athens. Arachne hesitated for a moment, then recklessly declared, "Let the competition begin!"

And so the two women began to weave. Soon Athena's design appeared. It depicted the dire consequences that befall mortals who displease the gods.

Her design complete, the goddess turned to look at her opponent's loom. What she saw there displeased her even more. Arachne had chosen to show some of the gods and goddesses in irreverent and unflattering ways. Anger flashed from Athena's eyes as she spoke, "You did not heed my warning. As I am patroness of arts and crafts, I swear that you will regret forever your failure to do so."

With that, Athena touched Arachne. Instantly, the mortal's body shrank, her arms and legs became hairy, and she was transformed into a tiny spider. "Now," said Athena, "You will spin for all eternity as a reminder for those who are tempted to doubt the superiority of the gods or are foolish enough to challenge them." And to this day, she does.

Name_____

A Myth Mesh

The lovely Arachne spun this web, ensnaring many topics related to Greek myth and legend. First, release one to use as the topic of some careful research. Then, fill the web below with dates, names, and/or notes related to the topic you have chosen.

Pandora's Box
Cronos
Jason
Medea
Odysseus
Olympus
Charon
Iris
Cyclopes
Electra
Pegasus
Medusa
Atalanta
Minotaur
Perseus
Gorgons
Midas
Eurydice
Argonauts
Prometheus
Minos
Atlas
Titans
Centaurs
Narcissus
Trojan Horse
Helen of Troy
Golden Fleece

Name_____

Clean Sweep

> An **inference** is an educated guess based on facts or premises. In the inference process, reasoning is used to come up with a single judgment based on the available evidence.

Clear the cobwebs from your mind. Using the story of Arachne or any other Greek myth you have read, answer the questions below. The first one has been done for you.

1. What can you infer from this myth about the Greek attitude toward the inhabitants of Mount Olympus?

The Greeks believed that the gods and goddesses should be worshiped and respected. They felt that these deities could and did travel to earth— both to observe and to control events. They also felt that these deities had the right to punish irreverence.

2. What can you infer from the evidence presented in this myth about the purpose of Greek myths?

_____
_____
_____
_____
_____

3. What can you infer from this myth about the special powers gods and goddesses possessed?

_____
_____
_____

4. What can you infer about the human characteristics some gods and goddesses displayed?

_____
_____
_____
_____
_____
_____
_____

5. What can you infer about the influence of mythology on the English language? Give at least one specific example.

_____
_____
_____
_____
_____

6. What can you infer from this myth about the Greek view of **hubris**, exaggerated pride or self-confidence?

_____
_____
_____
_____
_____

Name_____

The Mything Link

Characterization is the creation or delineation of characters in a story or play. There are five methods of characterization. Consider, for example, the goddess Athena.

1. What the character says
   Example: "I do not feel that mortals should compare their work or their appearances too favorably with those of the gods and goddesses," said Athena.

2. What the character does
   Example: Because Athena was angry with Arachne for boasting about her skill in weaving, the goddess turned the unfortunate girl into a spider.

3. What other characters say about the character
   Example: "My daughter Athena is a worthy goddess of truth and wisdom and ably defends the Greek city that has been named for her," Zeus proudly asserted.

4. How other characters act toward the character
   Example: The people who had gathered to watch Arachne spin gasped in horror as they glimpsed the glow of anger in Athena's eyes.

5. What the author says about the character
   Example: Athena sprang forth fully grown and in complete armor from the forehead of her father Zeus.

Greek myths developed at a time when there were few scientific explanations for everyday occurrences. In contrast, we live in an era that has produced an abundance of factual accounts and technical interpretations for common events; yet, some phenomena remain unexplained. For example, although scholars have advanced theories, we do not fully understand black holes, UFOs, or the strange disappearances of airplanes and ships in the Bermuda Triangle.

Create your own myth to account for some phenomenon science has not yet fully explained. Involve a well-known Greek god or goddess and one or more mortals in a plot that explains this phenomenon in mythological style. Use at least three methods of characterization to delineate your characters.

Name_____

Echo

Echo, a young wood nymph, was as flawless as the wildflowers she loved to pick. While her physical beauty was much admired, the musical quality of her voice attracted even more notice. As she frolicked through the woods each day, happiness surrounded her.

One morning as Echo was gathering some of the ferns that carpeted the forest floor, she was astonished to see Zeus run past her, accompanied by a young woman. Undetected, Echo watched in silence until the god and his companion had disappeared from sight. Then, she returned to her task.

Now Zeus's wife Hera was well known for her vengeful and jealous nature, so Echo was understandably upset to see her approaching in a very agitated state. To protect the ruler of the gods, Echo began a stream of chatter designed to delay the suspicious wife and to give her fiery anger time to cool. Instead, the ploy infuriated Hera, who vowed to punish Echo for her interference.

"Echo, you are impudent and unwise. Because you prevented me from finding my husband, you must pay dearly for your folly. From this day forward, you shall speak only when spoken to. You shall repeat what is said to you. Never again will your words be your own," Hera declared to the horrified nymph.

Echo was devastated by the unjust punishment Hera imposed on her. By Hera's command, Echo's greatest gift, her voice, had been rendered all but useless.

Echo forgot her sorrow, however, on the day she chanced to meet Narcissus, a handsome lad who was known to spurn the attentions of even the most beautiful maidens. Echo fell madly in love with him. This emotion, totally new to the young wood nymph, gave her shattered life purpose and hope. She raced to Narcissus, intent on expressing her fondness for him.

"Who are you?" he asked.

"Who are you?" she repeated.

"What are you up to?" he questioned, wrinkling his brow.

"What are you up to?" she replied.

Stamping his foot in consternation, Narcissus commanded, "Stop that!"

"Stop that," Echo replied woefully, as she began to realize the futility of her situation.

Infuriated by Echo's constant mimicking, Narcissus ordered her from his sight. "And don't ever come near me again," he concluded as he dashed away from her.

Poor Echo ran off in shame and hid in a cave for days. Grief stricken, she wasted away, until nothing was left but her lovely voice.

Name_____

Narcissus

Narcissus was a handsome lad, known to spurn the attentions of even the most beautiful maidens. His brazen and callous attitude did not go unnoticed on Mount Olympus. Of all the gods and goddesses, Aphrodite, the goddess of love, was most incensed by his selfish indifference. When she could no longer tolerate his egotism, she decided to punish him. He was to endure the same suffering he had inflicted upon those who had sought his love.

One day, as Narcissus ambled aimlessly through the woods, he happened to stop at the edge of a small pool. Chancing to look down, he caught his breath. There before him was a face whose beauty surpassed all he had seen before. Having, at last, encountered a visage he considered worthy of his affection, he fell hopelessly in love; but each time he reached down to touch the lovely countenance, it disappeared in a swirl of rippling water. For the first time, Narcissus knew the awful ache of unrequited love: he could not take his eyes off his own reflection. Day after day, he stood rooted to that spot. Oblivious to his need for sustenance, Narcissus soon pined away and died.

Upon learning of Narcissus's death, the wood nymphs hastened to the spot where he had died, intending to prepare his body for the funeral. Yet, as he had avoided them in life, so he eluded them in death. Where they had expected to find his body, they actually found only one delicate white flower. Even now, this flower bears his name—the narcissus.

Name_____

How's That Again?

> To **compare** is to show the ways in which similar things are alike or different. To **contrast** is to show the ways in which unlike things are different.

How an Echo Is Produced

Hikers are often enchanted to discover a picturesque spot in the mountains where they can call out across a valley and hear their own words come back to them. The explanation for this phenomenon is simple.

The human voice produces sounds that travel through the air in waves similar to the ripples created in still water when a stone is dropped into it. Normally, these waves spread out from the sound source, becoming weaker and weaker until they can no longer be heard at all. However, if these waves strike something smooth and hard, such as a stone cliff, they may bounce back. Returning in the direction from which they came, they produce an audible echo.

Compare this scientific explanation for an echo with the mythological account given on page 31. On the lines below, list ways in which these two accounts are similar and ways in which they are different.

Similarities

1. _____

_____

2. _____

_____

Differences

1. _____

_____

_____

_____

2. _____

_____

_____

_____

Myth Imagery

Figurative language is any language that is used creatively and imaginatively to evoke vivid images and to give fresh insights. There are several different types of figurative language.

1. In a **simile,** the word *like* or *as* is used to compare two things.
   Example: Her words were like an echo, repeating again and again in my troubled mind.

2. In a **metaphor,** a word or phrase literally denoting one kind of thing is used in place of another kind of thing to suggest a likeness or make a comparison between the two.
   Example: The mountain was Olympian in its grandeur.

3. In **personification,** human qualities are given to traits or to inanimate objects.
   Example: As queen of the gods, Hera should have felt free, but she was imprisoned by her own jealousy.

Look for examples of each of these types of figurative language in the myths about Arachne (page 27), Echo (page 31), Narcissus (page 32), Phaethon (pages 36–37), Persephone (page 42), Prometheus (page 44), Io (page 48), Bellerophon and Pegasus (page 51), Icarus and Daedalus (pages 57–58), Perseus (pages 61–63), or Heracles (pages 68–69). Write one example of each type on the lines below, and indicate where you found each example by recording the myth title and page number in parentheses after it.

1. *Simile:* _____

   _____

   _____

2. *Metaphor:* _____

   _____

   _____

3. *Personification:* _____

   _____

   _____

On the lines below, create and label your own example of one of these types of figurative language.

4. _____ : _____

   _____

   _____

Name_____

Olympian Analogies

An **analogy** is a relationship or correspondence between one pair of terms that serves as the basis for the creation of another pair. The terms in the second pair have the same relationship to each other as do the terms in the first pair. Some possible relationships are:

1. One word is a synonym for the other.
Example: Pride is to hubris as god is to deity.
2. One word is an antonym of the other.
Example: Proud is to modest as young is to old.
3. One word is a characteristic part of the other.
Example: Mast is to ship as wheel is to chariot.
4. One word is a kind of the other.
Example: Zeus is to Greek deity as Jupiter is to Roman deity.

Test your ability to recognize the relationships between words by completing these analogies. Write one word from the box on each line below, but be careful. There are more words in the box than you will need.

1. Gaea is to earth as _____ is to heaven.

2. Neptune is to Poseidon as _____ is to Ares.

3. Daedalus is to Icarus as _____ is to Phaethon.

4. Voice is to Echo as _____ is to Narcissus.

5. Labyrinth is to maze as _____ is to footrace.

6. Vulcanize is to raw rubber as _____ is to glass or steel.

7. Herculean is to tremendously difficult as _____ is to daringly original.

8. Enmity is to love as _____ is to honor.

9. Telephone is to sound as _____ is to sight.

10. Omniscient is to ignorant as _____ is to weak.

11. Mammal is to human being as _____ is to spider.

12. Winged sandals are to Hermes as _____ is to Poseidon.

13. Logotype is to corporation as _____ is to god.

14. Odyssey is to journey as _____ is to giant.

15. Choros is to Greek drama as _____ is to American play.

appearance	Helios	Mars	Poseidon	television
arachnid	ignominy	Mercury	Promethean	temper
attribute	Jupiter	narrator	run	titan
fame	maiden	Olympian	symbol	trident
flower	marathon	omnipotent	telegraph	Uranus

Phaethon

Phaethon lived with his mother and sisters in a tiny Greek Village. Though mortal, he had known from early childhood that he was the son of Helios, god of the sun. The boy was proud of his lineage and spoke of it frequently. Eventually, his companions tired of hearing his boasts. They ridiculed his claims, demanding proof that Helios was, indeed, his father.

For a time, Phaethon ignored their taunts; but finally, he could bear them no longer. He decided that he must take action: he'd visit his father in the Kingdom of the Sun and return with the proof his playmates desired. Having convinced his mother that his decision was wise, he departed.

The journey to the Kingdom of the Sun was a long and arduous one, and the boy was weary when he reached Helios's court. His exhaustion vanished, however, when he beheld Helios seated on his luminous throne, surrounded by kingly splendor. Phaethon stood there in silence until his father spoke. "Welcome, Phaethon," Helios said. "I am pleased to see what a fine young man you have become. But tell me, why have you made such a long and difficult journey?"

As the boy explained, Helios was moved by his obvious distress and rashly promised to grant him anything he wished. The god was astonished when Phaethon said, "Grant me the privilege of driving the chariot of the sun on its journey across the sky tomorrow." In vain, Helios tried to dissuade the boy, explaining that the journey was a treacherous one and that sometimes even he had difficulty controlling the horses. Phaethon remained adamant; and, at length, Helios acquiesced and led him reluctantly to the stable.

Phaethon
(continued)

Phaethon was filled with excitement. He could envision his friends watching in awe as he passed overhead; and the sight of the huge, fire-snorting horses did little to dampen his enthusiasm. Helios rubbed the boy's hands and feet with a linament to protect them from the incredible heat, harnessed the horses to the chariot, and helped Phaethon aboard. Then he handed the boy the reins, wishing him well.

Immediately, the chariot shot out of the stable, for the horses sensed that their driver was inexperienced. Frantically, Phaethon tried to bring them under control, but they darted erratically about—one moment racing heavenward, the next swooping down toward the earth.

On earth, people watched in terror as the sun rose in the sky and then abruptly dropped from view. As it disappeared, they felt frost and ice descend. The next moment, the sun reappeared and moved ever closer to earth. Trees and bushes were parched. Animals and people were singed. In an instant, vast deserts replaced grassy plains. Entire swamps were left arid. Mountains exploded, and rivers and lakes disappeared.

High on Mount Olympus, the gods watched, at first bemused and then concerned. Finally, Zeus decided that he must take action. He hurled a lightning bolt at the youth, who fell from the chariot and plunged to earth, his hair aflame. Meanwhile, the horses, tired from their wild exertions, returned to their normal path and sedately continued their appointed journey.

On earth, Phaethon's mother and sisters were inconsolable. They wept continually near the spot where Phaethon had fallen. Eventually, the gods took pity on them, and turned them into willow trees so that they might stand, forever weeping, near the youth's grave.

Special Effects

> The **effect** is what happened as the result of something; the **cause** is the reason for what happened.
>
> *Example:* Because Phaethon grew weary of being teased by his playmates, he decided to visit his father, Helios.
> *What happened?* Phaethon decided to visit Helios.
> *For what reason?* He was tired of being teased.

The drawings below and on page 39 show some of the causes and special effects of Phaethon's rash journey. Write a cause-and-effect statement for each one. The first statement has been written for you.

1. *Because Phaethon boasted often of his lineage, his playmates demanded proof that he was, indeed, the son of Helios, god of the sun.*

_____

3. _____

_____

_____

2. _____

_____

_____

_____

4. _____

_____

_____

_____

Special Effects
(continued)

5. _____
_____
_____
_____
_____

7. _____
_____
_____
_____
_____

6. _____
_____
_____
_____
_____

8. _____
_____
_____
_____
_____

An Amazing Quest

Greek and Roman mythology and the Greek and Latin languages have had an extensive influence on English. Many of the words we use today are direct borrowings or derivations from these sources. Read these sentences. Then go on a quest for the words you need to complete them by looking in dictionaries and encyclopedias. Write the correct words on the lines.

1. The **marathon** is named after a plain in Greece where the Greeks defeated the

_____.

2. _____, an English adjective meaning "daringly original or creative," comes from the name of **Prometheus**, the mythological hero who brought fire to earth in defiance of Zeus's order.

3. If you have ever been **panicked**, you'll know how Greek travelers felt when they were startled by _____, the Greek god of flocks and shepherds who was a son of Hermes.

4. The English word **zephyr**, meaning "a soft wind," comes from *Zephyrus*, the name given by the Greeks to the _____.

5. **Morpheus**, the son of Sleep and the god of dreams, gave his name to the painkilling drug _____.

6. The English word **dactyl**, meaning "a poetic foot consisting of one long syllable and two short ones," comes from the Greek word *dactylos*, meaning "_____."

7. The Greek word *hypokrites* means "actor" or "one who plays a role." What English word is derived from this Greek word? _____

8. **Calliope** was the Greek Muse of epic poetry. What is called by her name today?

_____

9. What **tantalized** poor Tantalus? _____

_____

_____

An Amazing Quest
(continued)

10. **Hyper** is an English prefix borrowed directly from Greek. What does this prefix mean?

    _____

11. *Museum* is a Latin word meaning "a place for learned occupations." From what other

    word is it derived? _____

12. The Latin word **caput** means "head." In Greek architecture, you'll find a **capital** at the

    _____ of each column.

13. Could you sit in a Greek **stadium**? _____ Why or why not? _____

    _____

14. In Greek, **amphi** means "on both sides"; therefore, an **amphitheater** is a theater with

    _____. In an amphitheater, tiers of seats are arranged around an

    open space. Amphitheaters are usually _____or _____in shape.

15. The Latin Word **orare** means "to speak, especially in a pleading or praying manner"

    and is closely related to the English word **oracle.** What was the role of the oracle in

    Greek mythology? _____

    _____

    _____

    What does this word mean today? _____

    _____

    What is a synonym for it? _____

16. To what geometric shape does the **Pythagorean** theorem apply? _____

    By whom was this theorem derived? _____

17. Is a bank vault intended to be **hermetic**? _____Explain your answer. _____

    _____

18. In Greek drama, the **choros** played a most important role. What did it do? _____

    _____

19. In Greek mythology, the twelve sons and daughters of Uranus and Gaea were called

    the **Titans.** These enormous beings of incredible strength deposed Uranus and later

    joined Cronos in battling Zeus and the Olympians for control of the universe. The

    Greek adjective **titanikos** means "of the Titans." What does the English adjective

    titanic mean? _____

    _____

orare · titanikos · choros

Persephone

Demeter, a daughter of Cronos and Rhea, was goddess of the earth's fruits. She determined what crops would grow and when harvests would be bountiful. By her brother Zeus, she became the mother of a daughter, whom she named Persephone.

Persephone spent many happy childhood hours frolicking in the sun and picking flowers in the meadows. In time, she grew to be a lovely young maiden. One day, when she was gathering blossoms on the Nysian plain in Asia, the earth beside her suddenly opened to reveal Hades, king of the lower world. Giver of all blessings from within the earth and god of wealth, Hades kidnapped the frightened maiden and carried her to his dark kingdom in a blackened chariot.

When Persephone did not return home at the end of the day, Demeter became worried and went looking for her. Frenziedly, the goddess searched the meadows and plains. Frantically, she entreated other gods and goddesses to tell her what they knew about Persephone's mysterious disappearance. At last, Helios took pity on the distraught mother and told her that it was Hades who had carried Persephone away.

Relieved to learn of her daughter's whereabouts, Demeter immediately went to Zeus to seek his help in securing Persephone's safe return. To the goddess's surprise and dismay, Zeus confessed that he had promised their brother Hades that he could have Persephone to be his wife. Thus, in kidnapping Persephone, Hades had only taken what was rightfully his and had done nothing wrong. For this reason, Zeus refused to intervene in the matter.

When Demeter learned that Zeus had made such a promise without telling her, she became extremely angry. In fact, she was so angry that she left Mount Olympus and refused to allow the earth to produce any fruits. Where once flowers and grain had been tossed by gentle breezes, brown stubble now stood stiffly. Zeus sent rain upon the earth to water the meadows and fields until they were muddy, but still nothing grew.

When Zeus saw how the whole earth remained barren despite his efforts, he became concerned for the welfare of his world and those who dwelt in it. At last, he sent Hermes into the lower world to secure the release of Persephone and bring her back to her mother. Hades agreed to allow Persephone to return with the messenger but offered her a pomegranate to eat. Before the hungry girl departed, she consumed six seeds.

When Zeus learned that Persephone had eaten in the lower world, he ruled that she would have to spend six months of each year with Hades. While Persephone is with Demeter, plants grow, bloom, and bear their fruit. When she returns to the darkness of the lower world, plants become dormant, and crops do not grow. And so it is that the earth experiences spring and summer, fall and winter.

Pick a Purpose

> The **author's purpose** is his or her intent in writing a piece of prose or poetry. It may be primarily to **describe**, to **entertain**, to **inform**, or to **persuade.**

1. Review the myth about Persephone on page 42. When it was first told many years ago in ancient Greece, its purpose was primarily to **inform** by explaining the seasons and the natural cycle of growth, dormancy, and regrowth. Today, because we understand the seasonal cycle in scientific rather than mythological terms, its primary purpose is to **entertain.**

2. Pretend that you are a close friend of Demeter's. On a separate sheet of paper, write an essay or journal entry in which you **describe** her grief upon learning of her daughter's disappearance.

3. Pretend that you are a newspaper reporter in ancient Greece. On a separate sheet of paper, write an article to **inform** your readers about Persephone's mysterious disappearance. Mention Hades' alleged role and Demeter's reaction. Arrange an interview with at least one of the gods or goddesses involved, and quote this deity in your article.

4. Pretend that you are the distraught Demeter. On a separate sheet of paper, write a letter in which you try to **persuade** your brother Zeus to help you secure the release and safe return of your daughter Persephone.

Name_____

Prometheus

Prometheus looked down from Olympus and was saddened by what he saw. Men, women, and children huddled together in the dark caves they inhabited, desperately trying to keep warm. What was even worse, they ate their food raw because they lacked the means to cook it. "This state of affairs must be changed," he thought to himself.

Prometheus believed that the gift of fire could change the lives of the people on earth. No longer would they be forced to dwell in cold darkness and eat raw food. Instead, they would have light and heat, and they would be able to cook. Pleased with himself for thinking of an answer to their dilemma, Prometheus searched throughout Olympus until he found Zeus.

"Great Zeus," Prometheus exclaimed, "look at the world you have created and see the crude state in which these mortals dwell. I wish to give them the gift of fire, that they may have light and heat and power."

"Prometheus, you fail to see the whole picture. The earth-dwellers are not unhappy with their lot. They live an innocent, satisfied existence. If you introduce fire, you will only bring danger and worry to a trouble-free world. Your beneficence may well be resented by those whom you seek to aid. I forbid you to give it to them!" bellowed Zeus as he turned his back and walked away, dismissing a stunned Prometheus.

The would-be bearer of gifts was angered by this curt reply. "I'll not take 'no' for an answer," he muttered under his breath. And with that, he raced away from Olympus, stopping only long enough to grab a huge torch.

When Prometheus arrived on earth with his glowing gift, those who were watching backed away from it until Prometheus assured them that it could be tamed. "Control it with water," he told them. As Prometheus was leaving to return to Olympus, he threw some raw meat onto the fire. The enticing aroma of cooking food enabled even the most reluctant onlookers to overcome their hesitations. Fire was, indeed, a welcome gift.

Not long afterward, Zeus looked down at the world and was shocked to see light. He could hear meat crackling on spits and smell the smoke of many blazes. "I have been defied," he stormed.

Zeus surveyed his kingdom until he spied the one he sought. Throwing his famous thunderbolt, he paralyzed Prometheus. "You have ignored my wishes, and for this you shall be punished!" roared the chief of the gods. "I banish you to the Caucasus Mountains, where you shall be chained to a rock. By day, an eagle will pick and tear at your liver, which shall be restored during each succeeding night. In this way, your torment will be unending. Never again shall you know peace and comfort." With that, Prometheus was led away to his place of punishment.

Name_____

A Case of Mythtaken Identity

> **Characterization** is the creation or delineation of characters in a story or play. There are five methods of characterization:
> 1. what the character says,
> 2. what the character does,
> 3. what other characters say about the character,
> 4. how other characters act toward the character, and
> 5. what the author says about the character.
> (For a more detailed explanation of **characterization** with examples, see page 30.)

The gods and goddesses on Mount Olympus are understandably confused. Two young men, both claiming to be Prometheus, have appeared before the Olympian council and demanded recognition. You have been asked to determine which one is the real Prometheus and which one is an imposter.

First, read the myth on page 44. Next, use statements in this myth to fill in the Personality Profile below. Then, turn to page 46 and read the accounts each suitor has given of a recent meeting with Artemis. Finally, make your determination. Is the real Prometheus Suitor A or Suitor B?

Personality Profile		
Personality Trait	**Method of Characterization**	**Textual Evidence**
caring	*what the character says*	*"'This state of affairs must be changed,' he thought to himself."*
cleverness		
		"Pleased with himself for thinking of an answer to their dilemma, Prometheus searched throughout Olympus until he found Zeus."
	what another character says	
rebelliousness		

A Case of Mythtaken Identity
(continued)

Read the two accounts below. On the basis of these accounts and the Personality Profile on page 45, decide which suitor is the real Prometheus. Indicate your choice by putting an **x** in the box beside his picture at the top of his account. Then, to prove that you are not "mythtaken," underline the statements in his account that support your choice.

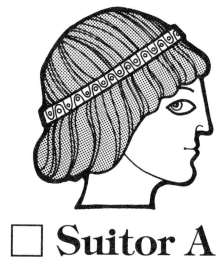

☐ **Suitor A**

☐ **Suitor B**

One day, while I was wandering through the forests on earth, I spied the goddess Artemis pursuing a young boy. The youth looked thoroughly frightened. He plunged recklessly through the brush, followed closely by Artemis and her hounds. Horrified, I called to the goddess. With obvious reluctance, she stopped and turned toward me. "Why are you chasing this lad?" I asked. "He's only a child!"

Scowling, Artemis replied, "The fool happened upon me as I was bathing and must now pay the price. I intend to turn him into a stag to provide sport for my hounds." She turned brusquely to continue the hunt, but the boy had fled. Furious, Artemis stalked off, determined to return the next day and complete the job.

I was trembling. Something had to be done, but I was fearful of Artemis's powers. Neither man nor god was immune to her anger. I thought for a time about what to do. Finally, I decided to leave the matter in the hands of the most wise Zeus. I flew quickly to Olympus, where I met with the king of the gods. He promised to talk with Artemis when she returned. Much relieved, I left, satisfied that a tragedy had been averted.

One day, while I was wandering through the forests on earth, I spied the goddess Artemis pursuing a young boy. The youth looked thoroughly frightened. He plunged recklessly through the brush, followed closely by Artemis and her hounds. Horrified, I called to the goddess. With obvious reluctance, she stopped and turned toward me. "Why are you chasing this lad?" I asked. "He's only a child!"

Scowling, Artemis replied, "The fool happened upon me as I was bathing and must now pay the price. I intend to turn him into a stag to provide sport for my hounds." With that, she turned brusquely to continue the hunt, but the terrified boy had fled. Furious, the goddess resolved to return the next day and finish the job.

I was horrified and knew that I had no time to waste. Quickly, I flew to Olympus, where I demanded an immediate audience with Zeus. The king of the gods listened, then said that he would talk with Artemis when she returned. He smiled and assured me that, by morning, she would have forgotten the whole thing. With that I left, outwardly calm but inwardly seething. I knew Artemis's rages—and her tenacity—only too well.

I returned to earth, where I found the youth cowering in his cottage. With a wave of my hand, I transformed him into a shining constellation and placed him in the sky. Now he will always be safe from Artemis and will serve as an eternal reminder of my concern for mankind.

Name_____

Cross Fire

> A **fact** is a statement that has been or can be proved to be true.
>   *Example:* People warm themselves with fire.
> An **opinion** is a statement that is believed but cannot be proved.
>   *Example:* Fire is good.

In giving fire to the earth-dwellers, Prometheus defied Zeus. Pretend that, rather than punishing Prometheus directly, Zeus has filed charges against him in a court of law. Prometheus has enlisted the services of a lawyer, Ms. True R. False. Each statement she makes is a fact. Zeus is represented by Mr. B. Lief, an attorney who spouts nothing but opinions. The case is now being heard by Judge For Yourself.

On the lines below, write a brief transcript of this hearing. Bear in mind the types of statements each lawyer would be likely to make. If you need additional space, continue on a separate sheet of paper.

Ms. True R. False: *Your honor and ladies and gentlemen of the jury, my client Pro-metheus is here to answer the charges that have been brought against him in this court of law.*

Mr. B. Lief: *Your client's actions are nothing short of abominable. He has stolen fire from heaven and used it to ruin life on earth!*

Ms. True R. False: _____

_____

_____

Mr. B. Lief: _____

_____

_____

Ms. True R. False: _____

_____

_____

Mr. B. Lief: _____

_____

_____

Judge For Yourself: _____

_____

_____

Name_____

Io

Hera was known, both on Olympus and on the earth, for her incredible jealousy. Though secure as the queen of the gods, she nevertheless flew into violent rages whenever she spied her husband in the company of another woman. Because she was unable to avenge herself on Zeus, she vented her anger on his companions. Zeus soon learned that he must protect those with whom he spoke, and he became very cautious, always watching for the approach of his wife. Yet even Zeus could not anticipate her appearance, for Hera was cunning.

One spring day, Zeus stood in a meadow chatting with Io, a beautiful young maiden. Suddenly, he spied Hera moving toward them. Fearing that, in her rage, Hera would harm poor Io, Zeus quickly transformed the astonished maiden into a gentle, white cow. Unfortunately, Hera witnessed this transformation. In a sweet, deceitful voice, she praised the creature and then asked that Zeus give her the animal as a gift. Though dismayed, Zeus could do little but agree, and Hera triumphantly led the cow away.

Now Hera was determined that Zeus and Io would not meet again. She commanded Argus to keep watch over the cow into which Io had been metamorphosed. Argus was especially well suited for this task because he had one hundred eyes. Even when he slept, some of his eyes kept their vigil. Thus, Zeus was frustrated in his attempts to see the young woman or to return her to human form.

Finally, Zeus could bear it no more, and he sent for Hermes. The messenger god was a master of deception, and he willingly agreed to slay Argus. He flew to earth with his flute and began to play softly near the unsuspecting watchman. His music was so sweet and so compelling that soon, one by one, the eyes of the mesmerized Argus began to close. After many hours, the last eye closed. Hermes drew a knife and cut off Argus's head. Sensing that she was free at last, Io wandered away.

Hera was furious when she discovered that Argus was dead. First, she transplanted his many eyes to the tail of the peacock, her favorite bird. Then, she sent a gadfly after Io. In only a short while, the pain of this insect's bites drove poor Io mad, and she began to run wildly about. She ran for days, past the sea that would later bear her name (the Ionian Sea) and then into faraway lands. It was only when she reached the banks of the Nile River that she found rest, was reunited with Zeus, and recovered her original form.

Thesaurus Therapy

The Prometheus myth on page 44 contains some words that could prove troublesome to a young reader. Remedy this situation by using a thesaurus or a dictionary to provide simpler substitutes for each of the potentially difficult words listed below.

1. huddled _____

2. inhabited _____

3. dilemma _____

4. crude _____

5. mortals _____

6. innocent _____

7. satisfied _____

8. existence _____

9. beneficence _____

10. forbid _____

11. bellowed _____

12. stunned _____

13. curt _____

14. enticing _____

15. aroma _____

16. reluctant _____

17. torment _____

℞ **MOUNT OLYMPUS PHARMACY**

No. 136

Dr. Apollo

Thesaurus Tablets
Take one four times a day
to make reading easier.

Now, rewrite this myth for a second-grade audience using the words you have found. Once you are satisfied with your version of the myth, either provide illustrations and produce it in picture book form or tape record it for younger children and nonreaders to enjoy.

Name_____

Keep an Eye on the Future

> **Foreshadowing** is giving an indication or warning of what is to come so that the reader can anticipate the mood or action.

1. Do you read with your eyes open? What words in the first paragraph of the myth about Io on page 48 warn you about what may happen to this unfortunate companion of Zeus's?

_____

_____

_____

_____

_____

2. How might the myth have been different if Zeus and Io had heeded this warning?

_____

_____

_____

_____

_____

3. Be Argus-eyed. Add your own foreshadowing clue to the myth, one that would cause it to end differently.

Clue: _____

_____

_____

Where it should be inserted: _____

_____

_____

4. Write your new ending for the myth on the lines below.

_____

_____

_____

_____

_____

_____

_____

_____

_____

Bellerophon and Pegasus

Bellerophon was an attractive young man with a keen mind and many friends. Life seemed wonderful to him until the day he accidentally killed a Corinthian named Belerus. To atone for this murder, he went to Proetus, king of Argos. Bellerophon was welcomed by Proetus and spent many happy days in his company.

Antea, Proetus's wife, was enchanted with the young visitor and became angry when he rebuffed her. Piqued, she told her husband that she had been wronged by their guest. Proetus was understandably enraged, but Zeus's laws of hospitality made it impossible for him to kill a guest in his house.

After some thought, Proetus asked Bellerophon to deliver a message to his father-in-law, Iobates, the king of Lycia. Bellerophon cheerfully agreed, not realizing, of course, that the note instructed the king to kill its bearer: Bellerophon was carrying his own death warrant.

When Bellerophon reached Lycia, he immediately became involved in court activities. In fact, several days passed before he remembered his mission and delivered the note. By that time, Iobates was confronted by the same dilemma that Proetus had faced: he could not kill a guest. Convinced that the young man must die, however, the king asked Bellerophon to complete a difficult task for him—the killing of the Chimera.

It was with great reluctance that Bellerophon agreed, for the Chimera was a horrible, fire-breathing monster with the head of a lion, the body of a goat, and the tail of a dragon. In despair, Bellerophon sought the counsel of an oracle and was much encouraged when the oracle told him that he would be victorious in his battle with the Chimera if he could harness the winged horse, Pegasus.

Now, Bellerophon prided himself on his horsemanship, and he knew the device required to catch and tame this particular animal. He hastened to the altar of Athena to request the use of her golden bridle. The goddess's bestowal of this coveted gift was a sure sign of her support and of Bellerophon's eventual success.

Bellerophon found Pegasus, slipped the bridle in place, and climbed on the glorious steed. Back and forth across the sky they raced, a perfectly synchronized team. At last, confident of their superiority, Bellerophon set out in search of his prey and, swooping down from above, effortlessly killed the horrid Chimera with his arrows.

When Bellerophon returned, Iobates was angered by his success. The enraged king then sent his visitor on one formidable mission after another, but each victorious return brought him closer to the realization that Bellerophon deserved to live. Eventually convinced that the gods smiled on the young adventurer, the Lycian monarch allowed Bellerophon to marry his daughter and made him successor to his throne. Thus it was that Bellerophon lived happily for many years.

As time passed, Bellerophon became more and more sure of himself until, one day, he decided to fly upon Pegasus to the top of Mount Olympus, the home of the gods. To punish this impudence, Zeus sent a gadfly to sting the horse. The startled horse reared and threw its rider to earth. Lame and blind as a result of his fall, Bellerophon became a reminder to other proud people of the dangers inherent in flying too high or otherwise seeking to challenge the superiority of the gods.

Get on Your High Horse

The **climax** of a story is the turning point, the moment at which the conflict is resolved.

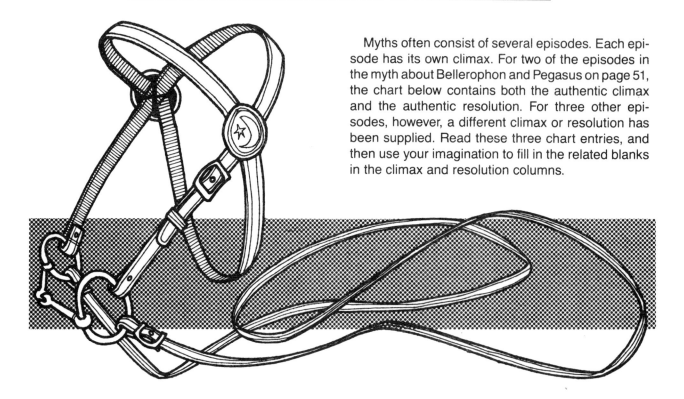

Myths often consist of several episodes. Each episode has its own climax. For two of the episodes in the myth about Bellerophon and Pegasus on page 51, the chart below contains both the authentic climax and the authentic resolution. For three other episodes, however, a different climax or resolution has been supplied. Read these three chart entries, and then use your imagination to fill in the related blanks in the climax and resolution columns.

Climax	Resolution
Bellerophon found Pegasus, slipped the bridle in place, and climbed on the glorious steed.	*They became a perfectly synchronized team.*
	Bellerophon, forced to seek medical attention for his injured thumb, was unable to kill the Chimera.
Pegasus bucked and threw Bellerophon off his back.	
The Chimera's roar frightened Pegasus.	
Zeus sent a gadfly to sting the horse.	*Bellerophon fell to the ground and was lame and blind as a result of the fall.*

Name_____

Riddled with Meaning

> Words with **multiple meanings** can be used in more than one way. For example, the word *run* is used in four different ways when we speak of a home *run*, a *run* in a stocking, and a *run* on a bank, or when we *run* a race.

Words with multiple meanings often form the basis for certain kinds of jokes. For example, the three riddles below all rely on words with multiple meanings for their humor. Read them, then write seven riddles of your own based on the words listed in the box at the bottom of this page or on other words with multiple meanings.

1. **Riddle:** *Why was Argus such a poor music teacher?* _____
   Answer: *Because he had too many* **pupils.** _____

2. **Riddle:** *When was Io in trouble?* _____
   Answer: *When she got an* **eyeful** *of Argus.* _____

3. **Riddle:** *Why was Hera such a dissatisfied wife?* _____
   Answer: *Because she couldn't* **cow** *Zeus.* _____

4. **Riddle:** _____
   Answer: _____

5. **Riddle:** _____
   Answer: _____

6. **Riddle:** _____
   Answer: _____

7. **Riddle:** _____
   Answer: _____

8. **Riddle:** _____
   Answer: _____

9. **Riddle:** _____
   Answer: _____

10. **Riddle:** _____
    Answer: _____

change	*low*	*pipe*
crop	*milk*	*quarry*
cross	*peer*	*switch*

Mood Ensemble

> **Mood** is the feeling an author wants to create for the reader. In a story, mood may be created by means of setting, situation, and description separately, or by any combination of these elements. In a play, mood is created by means of setting, situation, actions, and tone of voice. If the play has a chorus or narrator, description may also be used to create mood.

Materials Needed

enough copies of the myth about Bellerophon and Pegasus on page 51 for each member of the class to have one

Instructions

Preparation

1. Review the meaning of the word **mood** with the class.
2. Discuss the function of the chorus in Greek drama.
3. Read the myth about Bellerophon and Pegasus aloud, and discuss the way the mood changes as the myth progresses.
4. As a class, decide where dialogue might be appropriately inserted. For example, the first dialogue will probably be a conversation between Queen Antea and King Proteus in which she tells him that she has been wronged by Bellerophon.
5. On the chalkboard, list the conversations that should be included.
6. Divide the class into small groups, and ask each group to write one specific dialogue.
7. Type and photocopy a script that includes both the narration from page 51 and the dialogues written by the student groups.

Presentation

1. Distribute the scripts.
2. Cast the drama. Select five students to play the roles of Bellerophon, Proteus, Antea, Iobates, and Athena. Choose three students to narrate the pronouncements of the oracle. Ask the rest of the class to serve as members of the chorus.
3. Line up the chorus on stage, with individual actors in front and the oracles standing to one side in a group.
4. Explain that, while the chorus is speaking, the actors should remain still and that, when there is an interruption for dialogue, the chorus should freeze and remain motionless while individual actors speak.
5. Have the chorus members begin narrating the myth, speaking in unison and changing the tone of their voices to convey change in mood.
6. Have actors speak their parts in turn.

Follow-up

Have students perform their mood ensemble for another class or for their parents.

Name _____

Pygmalion and Galatea

> An **inference** is an educated guess based on facts or premises. In the inference process, reasoning is used to come up with a single judgment based on the available evidence.

Pygmalion was king of Cyprus. He fell in love with and finally married a maiden named Galatea. What can you infer from these pictures regarding the unusual circumstances surrounding their courtship? Write your answers on the lines under each picture.

1. What was Pygmalion's craft?

_____

_____

_____

3. How did Pygmalion feel about this statue?

_____

_____

_____

2. What unusual object did he create?

_____

_____

_____

4. What happened to the statue?

_____

_____

_____

Undercover Themes

> The **theme** is the subject or topic of a discourse or artistic representation. It is an idea about life expressed by an author or artist in a literary or artistic work.

Pygmalion and Galatea

Pygmalion was king of Cyprus. He was also an immensely talented sculptor. Working day after day in his studio, he created a marble statue of a woman. This statue was so captivatingly beautiful that Pygmalion fell in love with it. In fact, he was so strongly attracted to the ideal woman represented by his statue that he spurned the attentions and affections of all real women. In desperation, Pygmalion journeyed to Aphrodite's shrine, where he implored the goddess to breathe the breath of life into the cold, smooth, perfect form he loved. Aphrodite took pity on the handsome sculptor. Because she admired his loyalty to an ideal, she granted his request. Pygmalion returned to his studio and later married his marble-turned-maiden, whose name was Galatea.

When an author writes a story or, in the case of this myth, a storyteller tells a tale, the plot is shaped by the underlying theme he or she wishes to convey. In the myth about Pygmalion and Galatea, for example, the storyteller wants the reader to believe that loyalty to an ideal is a positive quality. Hence, he has Aphrodite reward Pygmalion for his steadfast devotion to the ideal woman he had created. If the myth had ended differently, the theme would have been different also. For each situation described below, uncover the theme and write it on the lines.

1. Pygmalion decided to leave the statue unfinished.

_____

_____

_____

2. After being brought to life by Aphrodite, Galatea decided that she did not like her creator, Pygmalion.

_____

_____

3. Instead of bringing Galatea to life, Aphrodite turned Pygmalion into a statue.

_____

_____

4. When Pygmalion returned to his studio after praying at Aphrodite's shrine, he found that the statue had been destroyed.

_____

_____

_____

5. Upon closer inspection, Pygmalion was amazed to discover that the statue he had so carefully created closely resembled a neighborhood maiden.

_____

_____

_____

6. The goddess Athena was jealous of Galatea and angry at Pygmalion for attempting to create ideal beauty.

_____

_____

_____

Name_____

Icarus and Daedalus

Daedalus was known throughout the Greek world for his ingenuity as an inventor. For the past few years, he had lived on the island of Crete, under the patronage of King Minos. This Minos was a cruel king. He kept a horrible beast called the Minotaur—a creature that was half man and half bull—on his island. To Daedalus, Minos entrusted the task of building a maze, or Labyrinth, to contain his fearsome pet. The maze Daedalus constructed was wonderfully intricate; and only the inventor, himself, knew how to escape from it.

Once a year, the barbaric king held a great celebration to honor the Minotaur. As a part of the festivities, seven Athenian youths and seven Athenian maidens were sacrificed to the beast. Because of the intricacy of Daedalus's maze, there was no escape for those who were chosen. They were led to the Labyrinth, soon became lost in its passageways, and wandered until they eventually reached the center, where they were devoured by the Minotaur.

This custom continued for many years until Theseus was chosen as one of the victims. Minos's own daughter, Ariadne, happened to see this young man as he was being paraded by, and instantly fell in love with him. She persuaded Daedalus to show her a way in which Theseus might escape from the treacherous maze. When the appointed day came, Theseus, carrying a ball of twine provided by Daedalus, made his way to the center of the maze, slew the Minotaur, and followed the twine back out. Then Ariadne, Theseus, and the Athenian youths and maidens escaped, leaving behind a furious King Minos.

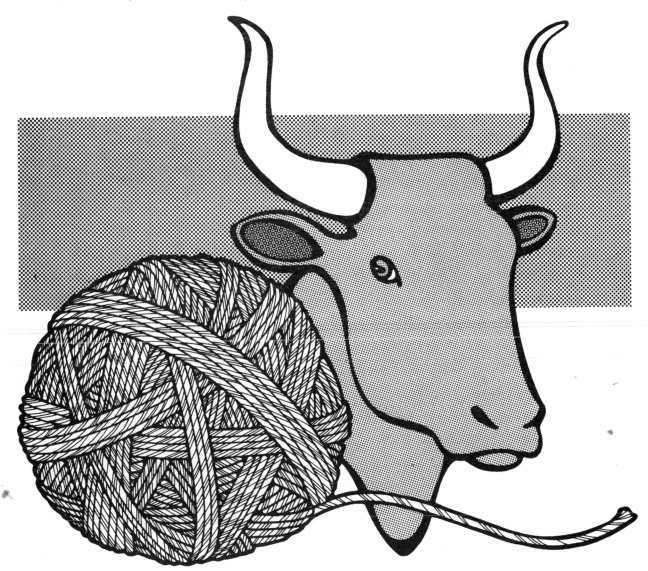

Icarus and Daedalus
(continued)

Sensing Daedalus's involvement in the escape, the angry Minos imprisoned the inventor and his young son, Icarus, in a tall tower on the edge of the sea. The drop-off was sheer, so escape was impossible.

The two lived together in the tower for several years until one day, while watching the seagulls swooping over the ocean, Daedalus had an idea. He set Icarus to work trapping gulls and plucking their feathers, while he built two wooden frames. When the frames were ready, Daedalus used hot wax to attach the feathers to them.

Father and son worked for weeks, until they had completed two perfect sets of wings. They would use them to escape from Crete, flying high above the heads of their captors.

When all was ready, Daedalus firmly cautioned his son. "Icarus," he said, "it is very important that you heed my words. Do not fly too high, for the sun will melt the wax that holds the feathers to the frame: do not fly too low, for the ocean spray will dampen the feathers and render the wings heavy and useless.

You must promise me faithfully that you will stay close and fly at the middle height." Icarus, who could scarcely contain his excitement, promised to obey his father's instructions; and they set out.

The wings Daedalus had so carefully constructed worked very well. The two soared through the air, elated with their freedom. Then Icarus, his head spinning with excitement, began to experiment. He whirled, dove, soared—moving quickly out of his father's reach. The helpless Daedalus could only watch anxiously as the happy boy cavorted.

Finally, with a cry of "Watch me, father. I can fly like the gods," Icarus soared upward. The hot sun, beating down on his wings, instantly melted the wax; and the feathers began to come loose and float in the air. With a scream, the boy plunged downward, falling headfirst into the sea, where he drowned. Grief stricken, Daedalus, made his way to the shore of Greece, where he mourned his son, gazing out over the waters known from that day to this as the Icarian Sea.

Name_____

Wing It!

Point of view is the voice the author uses to tell a story. It may be **first person,** in which the author is a character in the story and tells it from his or her point of view.
> *Example:* I could see by the wild look in the boy's eyes that my words of warning were going unheeded. Momentarily, I despaired; but the thought of freedom lifted my spirits.

It may be **third person objective,** in which the author is not a character in the story and is only able to report actions. This point of view is most often used in newspaper stories.
> *Example:* Icarus whirled, dove, and soared—moving quickly out of his father's reach.

It may be **third person omniscient,** in which the author is not a character in the story but is able to look into the characters' minds and to report what they are thinking.
> *Example:* Daedalus knew that his words of warning went unheeded. With a sigh, he continued his work, knowing that Icarus was thinking only about the exciting adventure that lay ahead and not about the dangers of escape.

Let your pen fly over the page as you write a first person account based on the myth about Icarus and Daedalus on pages 57 and 58. Be sure that you accurately portray the character you select. Your words should convey either Icarus's wild exuberance or Daedalus's anxiety and sorrow.

_____

_____

_____

_____

_____

_____

_____

_____

_____

If you need addiitonal space, use the back of this sheet or continue on a separate piece of paper.

Be a Synonym Seer

> **Synonyms** are words that have the same or very similar meanings. For example, *oracle* is a synonym for *seer.*

The words in this crossword puzzle have come into the English language from Greek. If, at first, it appears to be all Greek to you, don't despair. The synonyms will help you "see" the answers.

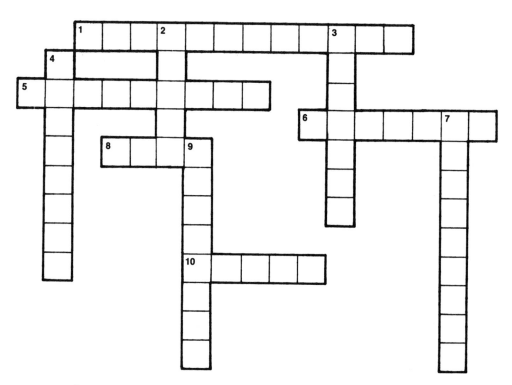

Across

1. Because Narcissus could not stop admiring himself, one synonym for conceited is _____.

5. A slave called a _____ escorted each Greek boy to school. Sometimes a teacher is called a _____.

6. A victorious athlete was crowned with the leaves of a small, evergreen plant. When one is content with his achievements, he is said to rest on his _____.

8. In Greek mythology, a nymph was condemned to repeat the words that were spoken to her. Today, a repetition of sound is called an _____.

10. Pan brought fear to the enemies of the Athenians. Today, debilitating fear is called _____.

Down

2. In Greek mythology, Clotho was one of the three Fates. Because she spun the thread of life, material woven of thread is called _____.

3. In Greek mythology, the Titans represented the uncontrollable forces of nature. Today, anything having great size, force, or power may be termed _____.

4. The Greek word for potter's clay is *ceramos.* From this word comes the English name for the potter's craft, _____.

7. King Minos asked Daedalus to build a _____ to hold the dreadful Minotaur. Today, an intricate maze is called _____.

9. Mount Olympus, the home of the gods, was always pictured as being high, distant, and cloud-enshrouded. Today, anything lofty and detached is said to be _____.

Name_____

Perseus

Though the prosperous Greek king, Acrisius, worshiped his beautiful daughter Danae, his yearning for a son prevented him from being completely happy. Eventually, he sought the counsel of the famed oracle at Delphi, who informed Acrisius that he would never have a son, but that he would one day have a grandson who would slay him. To prevent this appalling fate, the prophet warned, Acrisius would have to kill his daughter.

The king returned home and contemplated his dreadful dilemma for several days before coming up with an alternate solution that would enable him both to assure his own safety and to spare the life of his beloved daughter: he would see to it that she never married. Confining Danae to an underground prison with only her nurse for company would guarantee that the girl would have no contact with the outside world. There would be no entrance or exit, only a small hole in the roof through which food and drink could be passed.

Thus it was that Danae would have lived out her life had not Zeus chanced to pass overhead one day and to hear her singing. Enchanted, he came to earth to pay her a visit. Frustrated in his attempts by the impenetrable walls that surrounded Danae, the chief of the gods transformed himself into a golden rain shower and passed through the opening in the prison roof. After many happy visits, Zeus returned to Olympus, leaving behind a son named Perseus.

Stunned to learn that he had become a grandfather, Acrisius knew that the implications were clear: he must get rid of his daughter and grandson. Disconsolate, he ordered them sealed inside a huge chest and put to sea to drown.

Unbeknownst to the king, however, Zeus was watching this earthly drama. He kept vigil over mother and son until they reached the island of Seriphus, where he saw to it that they were dragged ashore in the net of Dictys, a kind fisherman who offered them a home. In Dictys's home, Perseus grew to be a fine, strong, young man, who watched over and protected his mother.

Polydectes, who ruled the island, was as unlike his brother Dictys as one could be. When Polydectes fell in love with Danae, he cared little that she did not return the sentiment. Certain that she would act differently if her son was not available to guard her, the cruel and selfish king sought a means by which he could rid the island of Perseus's presence. To that end, he planned a banquet to which each guest was expected to bring a worthy gift. Polydectes

Perseus
(continued)

demanded of Perseus that he bring the head of the Gorgon Medusa as his gift.

At one time, Medusa had been an attractive young maiden, but she had spent too much time admiring herself, especially her gorgeous hair. Finally, convinced that she was the most beautiful woman of all, she had grown too bold and had compared her beauty with that of Athena. In revenge, the goddess had turned the girl's hair into hideous snakes and had given her a gruesome face with bulging eyes and a protruding tongue. In fact, Medusa was so frighteningly ugly that all who looked directly at her were instantly turned to stone.

Zeus sent Hermes, the messenger god, to Perseus with some sage advice. Three items were essential to Perseus's success: the helmet of Hades, which would make the wearer invisible; winged sandals, which would make the wearer fleet of foot and able to fly; and a magic wallet, which could change size to accommodate anything that was put into it.

Hermes lent Perseus his own sword and Athena's shield for the venture, but informed Perseus that he would have to see the Graeae, three old women who were sisters of the Gorgons, to learn the location of the other articles he required.

Upon reaching the cave where the three old women lived, Perseus watched in amazement as they passed one eye back and forth among them. Realizing that the Graeae were forced to share this one eye in order to see, the young man instantly knew how he would force them to give him the information he sought. Dashing quickly into their midst from behind, he seized their single source of sight. Blind and desperate, the women begged for its return and readily agreed to the condition Perseus set: they would tell him where to find the objects he needed.

Following the directions that had been given to him by the Graeae, Perseus located the helmet, the sandals, and the wallet. At last, he was ready to undertake the task assigned him by King Polydectes.

Finding Medusa proved easy. Invisible because of the helmet he wore, Perseus swooped down on her undetected. Using the reflection in Athena's shield to guide him, he was able to cut off Medusa's head without looking directly at her. As he did so, he was astonished to see the winged horse Pegasus emerge from Medusa's neck and fly away.

His assignment completed, Perseus placed the severed head in his wallet and flew quickly toward home. Halfway there, he chanced to look down into a fabulously beautiful walled garden of trees loaded with golden apples. Intrigued, Perseus lowered himself into the orchard. As he looked about him in awe, he failed to hear the approach of Atlas, the master of

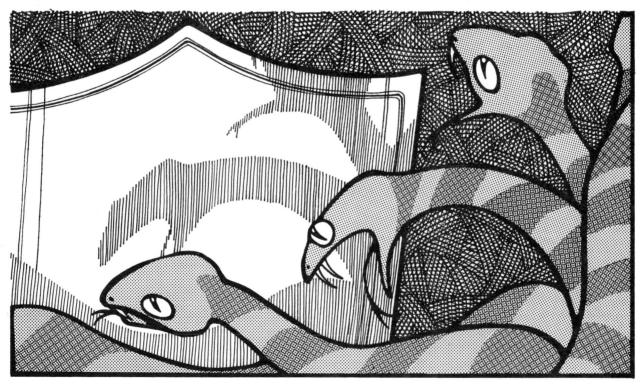

Perseus
(continued)

the gilded park. Seeking to diminish the offense caused by his trespassing, Perseus introduced himself as a son of Zeus and was dumbfounded by the response his doing so elicited. The giant, who had been warned that he would be killed by a son of Zeus, charged angrily toward his visitor. Perseus, knowing that he would be unable to defend himself adequately against so large an attacker, reached into the magic wallet, pulled out Medusa's head, and held it before Atlas. Immediately, the giant was turned to stone. A relieved but heavyhearted Perseus continued his journey home.

As he neared the coast, Perseus heard the distressed wails of a young woman and saw that a horrible sea monster was approaching her. Setting himself down near a group of horror-stricken spectators on the beach, Perseus learned that the young sufferer was Andromeda, whose mother had angered the gods by bragging of her great beauty. Ever since, the coast had been plagued by storms and sea serpents. Andromeda's father, the king, had been told that the only way to stop the punishment would be to sacrifice his daughter; thus, she was about to be devoured by one of these terrifying beasts. Perseus raced to slay the demon with Hermes' sword, then quickly freed Andromeda. After the two were married, they headed together for Seriphus to present Medusa's head to Polydectes.

Polydectes was shocked by the return of the young man who he had been so sure was dead. As the king was about to order his guards to kill the hero, he became fascinated by the wallet Perseus was holding. Slowly, Perseus drew out the head of Medusa and turned the king and all of his protectors into stone. At long last, he and Andromeda were free to return home.

Myth-Adventures

> The **plot** is the sequence of events in a story.

**Materials
Needed**
enough copies of the myth about Perseus on pages 61–63 for each member of the class to have one

Instructions
1. Review the meaning of the word **plot.**
2. Have all members of the class read the myth about Perseus.
3. Discuss the myth, noting its division into episodes and the use of the winged sandals, the helmet, and the magic wallet in these episodes.
4. Ask each student to write a new episode for the myth about Perseus.
5. Tell class members to use the first person point of view so that it will seem as if Perseus, himself, is recounting the events and to include winged sandals, a helmet, and a magic wallet as elements in their episodes.

Follow-up
One after another, have students read their episodes to the class. Then, bind the final drafts into a book called *The New Myth-Adventures of Perseus.* Keep this book for classroom use or donate it to the school library.

A Mythinterpretation

> The **denotation** of a word is its dictionary definition, its literal meaning. The **connotation** of a word is another meaning it suggests or the shading given its literal meaning by experience or association. For example, the denotation of the word *determined* is "unwavering or resolved." The denotation of the word *stubborn* is "fixed in purpose or course." While the denotations of these two words are similar, the word *stubborn* suggests "inflexible resolution"; hence, it carries a more negative connotation.

Anyone who reads the sentences below may mythinterpret Perseus's quest because of the connotations of some of the words that have been used. To avoid a mythinterpretation, translate these sentences into more neutral language. First, underline the word or phrase in each sentence that carries a negative connotation. Then, select a more neutral term from the box and write it at the end of the sentence. Be careful! You don't want to make a mythtake.

1. The ruthless King Polydectes taunted Perseus.

2. Perseus's obstinacy to prove King Polydectes wrong led him to agree to the dangerous quest.

3. After warning Perseus that he had made a rash promise to the king, Hermes gave him some sage advice.

4. The god of prudence and cleverness told the submissive Perseus how to overpower Medusa without being turned to stone.

5. Perseus's first task was to ferret out the Graeae, three old women who were sisters of the Gorgons.

6. Perseus persuaded the Graeae to help him by snatching the single eye that they were forced to share and over which they argued voraciously.

7. Perseus's success with the Graeae enabled him to continue his interminable quest for Medusa's head.

8. With the help of his magic shield, Perseus hacked Medusa's head from her body.

9. On his way back to King Polydectes, the vain youth rescued Andromeda from a sea serpent.

10. Andromeda's father felt that Perseus was merely a vagabond and would not bring his daughter happiness and wealth.

cut	eagerly	obedient	proud	unkind
determination	hasty	perpetual	search for	wanderer

A Heroic Leap in Time

> A **flashback** is an interruption in a story to permit the author to relate an event from the past.

Relax. This activity won't require Heraclean effort. The account of Heracles on pages 68–69 contains a flashback in which the hero's infancy and the events leading up to the first labor are recounted. Read it and then make your own heroic leap in time. On the lines below, list the events that the flashback would include if you began your account with the fifth labor, flashed back to Heracles' infancy, and then went forward through the last seven labors.

1. _____
2. _____
3. _____
4. _____
5. _____
6. _____
7. _____
8. _____
9. _____
10. _____
11. _____

If you are still confused about flashback, write a short, vivid account of *one* of the twelve labors. Begin your version with the *end* of the labor and flash back to the preceding events.

Name_____

Ferret out the Facts

> A **fact** is a statement that has been or can be proved to be true.
> *Example:* There is a myth about Heracles.
> An **opinion** is a statement that is believed but cannot be proved.
> *Example:* The myth about Heracles is the most exciting of all Greek and Roman myths.

Below is a list of statements. Some of these statements are facts, and some of them are opinions. Read them carefully. Then write an **F** on the line in front of each statement that is a **fact**, and write an **O** on the line in front of each statement that is an **opinion.**

_____ 1. First the Greeks and then the Romans told traditional stories called myths.

_____ 2. A Greek myth about Heracles says that he performed twelve labors.

_____ 3. Myths are fun to read.

_____ 4. Long ago, myths were one way of explaining natural phenomena.

_____ 5. Today, we have scientific explanations for many natural phenomena.

_____ 6. Because science has given us explanations, we no longer enjoy myths.

_____ 7. We can learn something about what the Greeks believed and what they valued by reading the myths they told.

_____ 8. The Greeks believed that the gods would not tolerate hubris.

_____ 9. The Greek gods would not tolerate hubris.

_____ 10. Spiders belong to a class of arthropods called Arachnida and are, therefore, sometimes termed arachnids.

_____ 11. Spiders and other arachnids are scary.

_____ 12. Echo was a beautiful young wood nymph with a lilting, musical voice.

_____ 13. An echo is the repetition of a sound caused by reflection of sound waves.

_____ 14. Prometheus was wrong to carry fire to the earth-dwellers in defiance of Zeus.

_____ 15. Fire has changed the lives of people on earth in many ways.

Heracles

Heracles was known throughout Greece as a great hero. His incredible strength was legendary, a blessing from the gods. Yet now, humbled by tragedy, he cursed his own power and marveled at how far he had fallen.

The son of a mortal woman and the god Zeus, Heracles had shown prodigious strength from birth. While yet an infant, he had easily strangled two serpents sent by the jealous goddess Hera to destroy him. As he grew, he had been instructed in chariot driving, wrestling, fighting in heavy armor, singing, and playing the lyre; and his strength had increased steadily.

When Heracles had reached eighteen years of age, he had married Creon's daughter Megara and had become the father of several children. For some years, he had known happiness, until Hera had cast a spell of madness upon him, and he had murdered his own children. In despair, he had sought the advice of an oracle, who had told him that his soul would not rest until he had done penance for their deaths. Thus it was that Heracles now found himself in the court of the wicked King Eurystheus.

Heracles listened as the king outlined his plan: "You are to perform twelve labors. If you complete them successfully, you will have atoned for the deaths of your children." The distraught hero agreed to the king's plan and set off on the first labor—to kill the Nemean lion and bring Eurystheus its skin. When Heracles came upon this hulking beast, it had just finished gorging itself on a kill. Realizing that his arrows were useless against such prey, Heracles stunned the creature with his club and then strangled it with his bare hands.

Heracles returned to court, where he showed the skin to the surprised king, who sent him to kill the Lernean hydra, a nine-headed swamp monster. The task proved to be a difficult one because each time Heracles cut off one head, two others grew in its place. It was only with the help of his faithful servant Iolaus that Heracles was able to dispatch eight of the heads and to bury the ninth, still living, under a huge rock.

Heracles
(continued)

The third and fourth labors were more easily accomplished. With the help of the goddess Artemis, Heracles pursued the Aracadian stag for more than a year, caught it, carried it home, and showed it to the astounded king. Likewise, Heracles destroyed the Erymanthian boar. For days, he tracked this beast through deep snow. When the animal was, at last, exhausted, Heracles hoisted it onto his shoulders and carried it to court, where the cowardly king hid himself in fear.

The fifth labor was to clean the stalls where Augeas, king of Elis, kept his three thousand oxen. To perform this seemingly impossible task, Heracles diverted two large rivers so that they would flow through the stables. He completed this labor in a single day and returned to court where Eurystheus, angered by Heracles' success, ordered him to kill the Stymphalian birds, bronze-clawed creatures that feasted insatiably on human flesh. With the help of a rattle given him by Athena, Heracles startled the birds and then shot them with arrows as they took flight.

This time, the furious king was determined that the strong mortal should fail, so Eurystheus sent Heracles to capture the mad Cretan bull kept in the Labyrinth by King Minos. The triumphant Heracles carried the fearsome beast, still living, home on his broad shoulders but then set it free.

Immediately, Eurystheus sent Heracles on another labor—the eighth—the capture of the meat-eating mares of Diomedes. During the ensuing battle, Heracles killed Diomedes and threw his body to the mares, which became tame after eating the flesh of their master.

Although Heracles was growing weary and longed for an end to his labors, at Eurystheus's command, he traveled to the land of the Amazons, where he charmed Queen Hippolyta into giving him her special belt. Unfortunately, the queen's followers were confused by Hera so that they misunderstood what Heracles was trying to do and attacked him. During the battle that followed, Hippolyta, herself, was killed. Filled with grief, Heracles returned again to King Eurystheus.

Labors ten and eleven were soon accomplished. First, Heracles killed the oxen of Geryones. Then, he traveled to the kingdom of the Hesperides for some golden apples, on the way freeing the bound Prometheus and tricking the Titan, Atlas. After the last and most difficult of the labors, a journey to the lower world to bring back Cerberus, the dog that guarded the entrance to this region, Heracles' penance was complete, and he returned home.

The Adventures of Odysseus

The episode below was taken from the story of Odysseus, a Greek hero whose wanderings were chronicled by the poet Homer. Because Odysseus had angered the god Poseidon, he was forced to journey for ten years after the end of the Trojan War before reaching his home in Ithaca at last. During this odyssey, he had a series of fantastic adventures. One of these adventures took place in the land of the Cyclopes.

The Land of the Cyclopes

Days passed. Though Odysseus and his men were relieved to have escaped from the land of the Lotus Eaters, their joy was dulled by incredible hunger: it had been many days since they had eaten. Suddenly, they spied a small island. Waves crashed against the rocky cliffs surrounding it, and goats grazed on the grassy plains at its summit. Quickly, Odysseus ordered the men to anchor the ship; and in an amazingly short time, a small party of sailors was scaling the steep stone walls.

When they reached the top, they smelled the enticing aroma of roasting meat emanating from a nearby cave. Before Odysseus could stop the starving sailors, they rushed headlong through the broad entrance and into the dark interior. Worried, their leader followed them, pleading for caution. Suddenly, a dark form loomed in the doorway. Too late Odysseus realized that this must be the island of the Cyclopes, three one-eyed giants who were the sons of Uranus and Gaea. This cave was the home of Polyphemus, a huge Cyclops; and it was he who stood blocking their escape. With a cruel chuckle, the titan herded the goats he had been tending into the cave and then rolled a gigantic boulder in front of the entrance.

Odysseus and his men ran frantically about, searching for places to hide; but their search was futile. With an effortless sweep of his enormous hand, Polyphemus plucked two men from the rocky floor of his cave and devoured them. Horrified, the Greek sailors hid themselves in recesses in the wall, hoping that the giant's hunger had been assuaged.

It was a long night. In the morning, the Cyclops once again led his herd from the cave, carefully rolling the huge boulder back in front of the entrance. Odysseus and his men waited until they were certain that the giant was well out of earshot. Then, they met in desperate council to devise a plan.

That evening, when Polyphemus returned to his

cave, Odysseus and his men were ready. Tremulously, Odysseus approached the giant, being careful to stand just beyond his lengthy reach. "Oh great titan," the Greek war hero said, "I have brought a present to you worthy of your power." With that, he motioned his men to bring forth a huge tub of wine. Now Odysseus knew that this wine was very strong—and it was very important that the giant drink it. He stood anxiously awaiting Polyphemus's response.

The giant frowned and then bellowed in a deep voice, "Why should I trust you? This could be a trick. I don't even know your name."

"My name?" answered Odysseus. "My name is 'No Man.' I'll prove that this is not a trick. I'll drink some of this heavenly wine myself." With much effort, Odysseus took a large gulp, passing the rest carefully to the Cyclops.

Some time and many tubs of wine later, the huge giant lay in drunken slumber, his snores reverberating throughout the cave. Quickly, Odysseus and his men heated a long log, which they had sharpened on one end; and then, with one firm blow, they thrust it into the Cyclops's single eye.

Instantly, the giant jumped up, shrieking in pain. With an awful wrench, he pulled the log from his eye, then fell to his knees, swaying and moaning. His cries reached the ears of his fellow Cyclopes, who came quickly to see why Polyphemus was making so much noise. They clustered outside the cave, calling, "Poly-

The Adventures of Odysseus
(continued)

phemus, has any man hurt you?" To their question the agonized titan replied, "No Man has hurt me." Satisfied that Polyphemus's agony was the will and work of the gods, the other Cyclopes moved away; and Polyphemus was left to suffer alone.

"Curse you, No Man," screamed the titan. "You have blinded me, but you will never leave my cave alive."

Odysseus and his men pressed themselves more firmly against the damp walls of the cave and waited for morning.

With the dawn, Polyphemus once again prepared to let his herd out to graze. Suspecting a trick and determined that no Greek should escape, he ran his hands over the back of each animal. In his blindness, he did not realize that the goats had been tied together in threes and that a sailor clung underneath the middle goat in each trio. Only by clinging desperately to the belly of the last animal was Odysseus, himself, able to escape.

Once outside the cave, Odysseus raced toward the beach, calling to his men as he ran. Meanwhile, Polyphemus had appeared on the promontory above Odysseus's head. The Greek war hero, exhilarated by his narrow but successful escape, could not resist taunting the huge creature. "Polyphemus," he called, "my name is Odysseus. If anyone asks who injured you, tell them that Odysseus of Ithaca was responsible." Then, with a joyous laugh, Odysseus clambered aboard the boat.

The enraged titan's response was to hurl a huge boulder toward the sound, narrowly missing the Greek ship. Then, as Odysseus and his men rowed frantically out of the harbor, Polyphemus raised his arms to the sky in supplication and begged his father, Poseidon, for revenge upon Odysseus. Instantly, a strong breeze sprang up; and once again, the small band of Greek sailors found themselves wandering far off course.

Set Sail for Adventure!

The **setting** is the time and place in which an event occurs.

Welcome aboard the *U.S.S. Odysseus,* a luxury liner that frequently sails in the Mediterranean, Ionian, and Aegean seas. A travel agent has created this appealing description of the Land of the Cyclopes, your next port of call. This description is designed to help you "sea" this setting in a positive and alluring way. Unfortunately, the agent had time to describe only one setting. Your help is needed to create a complete travelogue to advertise a voyage on which vacationers will follow the route taken by Odysseus on his journey home to Ithaca after the Trojan War and will visit each of his ports of call.

First, read the travel agent's description of the setting and activities planned for the fifth day of the journey. Next, read any account of Odysseus's wanderings. Then, write your own travelogue, carefully describing the setting for each one of Odysseus's adventures. When you have finished, select a format for your travelogue—brochure, pamphlet, poster, or scroll—and prepare it for display in your classroom.

DAY 5

We hope that you are still with us! Our journey continues to the Land of the Cyclopes. A gem of an island nestled in the blue Mediterranean, Sicily is lush and green with unsurpassed beaches. Goats graze peacefully on its emerald hillsides. Relax, walk about, or just sit on the craggy shore watching the waves crash against the rocks. A word of caution: The island's inhabitants are not particularly hospitable, so stick to the beaches and be ready to spring for the boat. The famous Cave Restaurant is closed at this time of year, so a beach barbecue will be provided. Bring a hearty appetite.

Extra! Extra! Read All About It!

To write the text for any paragraph, you need a topic, or **main idea,** and you need the details to support that idea. These **supporting details** clarify your meaning or idea and complete the word picture you are trying to create.

The presses are rolling. In the spaces below, create headlines for any eight of the thirteen myths you have read during this unit of study. Be sure that your words summarize the main idea of each myth and get the readers' attention!

Concern for Mankind Puts Prometheus on the Rocks

Theseus Amazes Everyone With Conquest of Minotaur

Name_____

The Two Frogs

Fables are short stories in which human weaknesses or faults are described primarily through the words and actions of animals. Although these stories are amusing, they have a serious purpose. They are intended to teach a useful lesson, or **moral.**

One of the most famous writers of fables was Aesop, a Greek slave reputed to have lived between 620 and 560 B.C. Because Aesop was fearful that his stories might offend the rich and powerful, he used animals to represent the human beings in them. So that no one would misunderstand his intent, he wrote the moral at the end of each fable.

The fables on this page and on page 75 were adapted from those supposedly written by Aesop more than two thousand years ago.

Once upon a time, two frogs were hopping wearily along a dusty road. It was August, and all around them the ground lay parched and bare. The ponds in which they usually swam had long since dried up, and the two had set out in search of water. Finally, they reached the edge of an old well. They peered down cautiously and were delighted to see cool, green water at the very bottom.

"At last!" exclaimed the one frog, and he readied himself for a leap into the well.

"Wait!" cried the other, an older and wiser fellow. "If you jump now, what will you do when this water, too, dries up? You will be trapped and will surely die. I think that we should continue on our way. We're bound to find safer water somewhere else."

The young frog thought for a moment, then sadly agreed; and the two hopped off into the distance.

Moral: Think twice before
you leap.

Name_____

The Sun and the Wind

The Sun and the Wind met one day in the heavens, and an argument began. "Poor Sun," said the Wind, "to be so large and yet so weak. I am clearly much stronger than you are."

To this the peaceful Sun replied, "That's simply not true," and he smiled benevolently at the Wind.

This only infuriated the Wind, who became more and more eager to prove his superior strength. "Look," he said at last, "a traveler is approaching. Let us find out once and for all who really is the stronger. We shall both try to remove that man's coat, and the one who succeeds in doing so will be acknowledged as the winner."

"Very well," agreed the Sun reluctantly.

The Wind summoned all of his strength and blew fiercely at the unsuspecting traveler. As the breezes swirled about him, the man's coat flapped wildly. With both hands, he clutched it tightly to his chest. The harder the Wind blew, the more firmly the man held the coat. Finally, the Wind stopped, out of breath and exhausted by his unsuccessful efforts.

Then the Sun smiled and beamed down upon the road. In only a few minutes, the grateful traveler was wiping his brow and removing his coat.

Moral: Gentleness is often more effective than force.

The Greedy Lion

It had been a long summer, and the animals were all very hungry. One day, after a futile hunt, the lion called a jackal, a fox, and a wolf to him. "Brothers," he said, "the hunting is poor, and we are all in danger of starving. Let us agree to help one another. Whoever finds game will share it with the rest, and thus we shall all survive." The other animals agreed to the plan and set off in search of game.

A short time later, the fox came upon a plump deer, which he stalked, killed, and dutifully brought back to the other animals. The lion was delighted and quickly divided the kill into quarters, according to the agreed-upon plan. Then he growled ferociously and said in his fiercest voice, "Now, the first quarter is mine—as my rightful share." The other three animals nodded, content with the agreement they had made. But the lion went on, "The second quarter is also mine, for I am the King of the Beasts. The third quarter I claim as my due, for I am the fiercest of all animals; and the last quarter is also for me because I will destroy any of you who attempts to take it from me."

With that, the greedy lion lay down and devoured the entire deer while the other three animals stood by, hungry and helpless.

Moral: Might makes right!

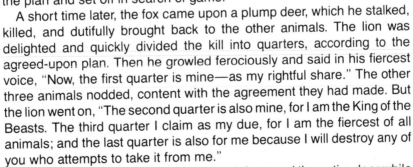

Fable Fun

The **author's purpose** is his or her intent in writing a piece of prose or poetry. It may be primarily to **describe,** to **entertain,** to **inform,** or to **persuade.**

Fables have traditionally been written to **inform** the reader about the consequences of a particularly foolish plan or course of action and to **persuade** him or her to reconsider or to take a different approach. The most well-known of the fable writers—the Greek slave, Aesop—fashioned his fables around animal characters in situations from which appropriate lessons, or **morals,** could be drawn. His purpose was to teach, rather than to describe or to entertain. The fable about frogs on page 74 is a typical example.

While Aesop's humorous fables had a serious intent, it is possible to write fables to amuse. For example, the tale that follows was written purely to entertain; any learning that the reader experiences is definitely unintentional! Read it, and then, on a separate sheet of paper, write your own just-for-fun fable to share with the class.

The Unhappy Lovers

One evening, a beautiful young maiden sat weeping by the side of a river. Suddenly, a kindly old frog spoke to her. "What's the problem?" he asked. "No one as lovely as you should be so unhappy."

"Oh," cried the girl, "I love the youth across the river, but we shall never meet. The river is too wide, and neither of us can swim. Our plight is hopeless."

The frog squinted and gazed to the far bank of the river. Sure enough, there sat a young man. "Well," declared the frog resolutely, "something must be done." With that, he gave a shrill whistle, and suddenly frogs' heads popped up all over the river, creating a veritable sea of green. The frog then told the surprised maiden, "I'll line up my fellow frogs, and you can walk lightly over their backs to reach the other side. But you must move quickly. Your weight is so much greater than ours that, if you pause too long, we shall not be able to support you." The girl was delighted; and casting a quick glance across the river, she started out.

At first, all went well, and the maiden was soon within three frogs' backs of the shore and true love. She could see the face of her beloved clearly. He was even more handsome than she had imagined. Lovesick, she stood transfixed, staring at his mesmerizing visage. The poor frog on whose back she stood began to sink slowly into the watery depths; and this story would certainly have had an unhappy ending if the kindly old frog on the far shore had not croaked loudly, "Jump! Jump!" Without thinking, the entranced maiden did as she was told and landed safely in the outstretched arms of her beloved.

Moral: Leap twice before you think!

Fable Figures

> **Figurative language** is any language that is used creatively and imaginatively to evoke vivid images and to give fresh insights. There are several different types of figurative language.
>
> **1.** In a **simile,** the word *like* or *as* is used to compare two things.
> *Example:* Her words were like an echo, repeating again and again in my troubled mind.
> **2.** In a **metaphor,** a word or phrase literally denoting one kind of thing is used in place of another kind of thing to suggest a likeness or make a comparison between the two.
> *Example:* The mountain was Olympian in its grandeur.
> **3.** In **personification,** human qualities are given to traits or to inanimate objects.
> *Example:* As queen of the gods, Hera should have felt free, but she was imprisoned by her own jealousy.

On the lines beside each sentence, write the two things that are being compared.

1. The prince was a jaguar, sleek and dangerous.   _____

2. He scanned the crowd carefully with the keen eyes of a hungry hawk on the hunt.   _____

3. The grateful Demeter grasped Persephone in the secure and loving hug of a koala.   _____

Complete these similes by adding references to the qualities or characteristics of particular animals. The first one has been done for you.

4. Icarus's joy was as overpowering as _*a lion's hunger*_____.

5. Arachne was as vain as _____.

6. Athena's eyes were as gray as _____.

7. Cronos was as grouchy as _____.

8. Zeus's anger was as violent as _____.

Complete these similes by adding nouns, common or proper.

9. _____ raced around like squirrels in his brain.

10. _____ groaned like an overstuffed hippopotamus.

It's Debatable

The **protagonist** is the leading character or hero of a story. The **antagonist** is an opponent, the adversary of the protagonist.

Materials Needed

one proverb for each student in the class
scissors
a widemouthed container
a speaker's stand or podium if available

Instructions

Before Class

1. Make several copies of the proverbs on page 94.
2. Cut these proverbs apart, noting that there are two versions of each one and that these versions are marked **A** and **P** for **antagonist** and **protagonist.**
3. Fold the proverbs and place them in the container, being certain to include both versions of each one.

During Class

1. Review the concept of **antagonist** and **protagonist** using any well-known fable. For example, "The Tortoise and the Hare" works quite well.
2. Have each student draw a proverb from the container.
3. Tell students to read their proverbs.
4. Explain what **A** and **P** stand for, and ask if there are any questions.
5. Tell students to work silently for twenty minutes preparing arguments in which they will either agree (as protagonist) or disagree (as antagonist) with the proverb. In their arguments, they are to state their position clearly and then to present four or more situations (real or hypothetical) supporting that position.
6. Review the debate format you will use. If time permits, you might follow these guidelines:
   a. The debate begins with the presentation of arguments by the protagonist, called the **protagonist construction,** for which the time limit is four minutes.
   b. The debate continues with the presentation of arguments by the antagonist, called the **antagonist construction,** for which the time limit is four minutes.
   c. After a two-minute break, the antagonist offers arguments challenging the protagonist's position in the **antagonist rebuttal,** for which the time limit is two minutes.
   d. Then the protagonist presents arguments challenging the antagonist's position in the **protagonist rebuttal,** for which the time limit is two minutes.
7. Have students follow the agreed-upon format as they present their arguments.
8. If possible have the debates scored by an impartial panel of three judges. If not, have class members vote after each debate to decide who has presented the stronger arguments.
9. On the basis of panel scoring or class vote, declare a winner of each debate.

Follow-up

After all of the debates have been presented, hold a runoff for the winners using different proverbs.

Name_____

Concrete Conclusions

Drawing conclusions means reaching a decision or making a judgment based on a body of evidence or a group of facts.

Often you can draw some very solid conclusions about a person or product based on its nickname. For example, what would you conclude about

1. a computer called the Elephant?

_____

2. a bike race called the Snail Classic?

_____

3. a woman referred to as a peacock?

_____

4. a sportscar called the Turtle?

_____

5. a child whose room is called the monkey cage?

_____

6. a sportscoat called the Parrot?

_____

7. a dentist called the Rabbit?

_____

8. a stock market that is bullish?

_____

On a separate sheet of paper, create product names for

- a terrifying amusement park ride.
- a physical fitness club.
- a new fast food restaurant.
- a homework machine.

Posttest

Match these terms with their definitions by writing the correct letter on each line.

____ **1.** analogy

____ **2.** antagonist

____ **3.** author's purpose

____ **4.** cause

____ **5.** characterization

____ **6.** climax

____ **7.** compare

____ **8.** contrast

____ **9.** drawing conclusions

____ **10.** effect

____ **11.** fact

____ **12.** figurative language

____ **13.** foreshadowing

____ **14.** inference

____ **15.** mood

____ **16.** opinion

____ **17.** plot

____ **18.** point of view

____ **19.** protagonist

____ **20.** sequencing

____ **21.** setting

____ **22.** symbol

____ **23.** theme

____ **24.** tone

A. an object, person, place, or event that can be used to stand for, represent, or suggest something else

B. the hero of a story

C. the intent of the writer; the reason for writing

D. the sequence of events in a story

E. the turning point of a story; the moment at which the conflict is resolved

F. clues the author provides to help the reader anticipate the action

G. the voice the author uses to tell a story

H. putting events, facts, or objects in some meaningful order

I. an opponent, or adversary

J. an educated guess based on facts or premises

K. the feeling an author wishes to create for the reader

L. a statement that has been or can be proved to be true

M. the style or manner of expression in speaking or writing, which reflects the author's attitude toward the spoken or written material

N. to show the ways in which unlike things are different

O. the time and place in which an event occurs

P. to show the ways in which similar things are alike or different

Q. any language that is used creatively and imaginatively to evoke vivid images and to give fresh insights

R. a statement that is believed but cannot be proved

S. reaching a decision or making a judgment based on a body of evidence or a group of facts

T. what happened as a result of something

U. the reason for what happened

V. the creation or delineation of characters in a story or play

W. a relationship or correspondence between one pair of terms that serves as the basis for the creation of another pair in which the terms have the same relationship to each other as do the terms in the first pair

X. the subject or topic of a discourse or artistic representation; an idea about life expressed by an author or artist in a literary or artistic work

Posttest
(continued)

Read each question below. Then write the correct answer on the numbered line.

25. When Greek myths were first told, what was their purpose?

25. _____

26. When Greek myths are read or told today, what is their purpose?

26. _____

27. Why has the purpose of Greek myths changed?

27. _____

_____

_____

_____

_____

_____

28. Complete the following analogy: <u>Zeus</u> is to <u>Greek god</u> as <u>John Glenn</u> is to _____.

28. _____

29. Write a synonym for the word <u>echo</u>.

29. _____

30. Write a synonym for the word <u>narcissistic</u>.

30. _____

31. What is the meaning of the root word <u>tele-</u>?

31. _____

32. What is the denotation of the word <u>ugly</u>?

32. _____

33. What is the name of a book that contains words and their synonyms?

33. _____

34. Is the following statement a fact or an opinion?

34. _____

Zeus was strong, mighty, and just.

35. Is the following statement a fact or an opinion?

35. _____

Zeus was a recognized member of the Greek pantheon.

Computer Challenge

```
10    PRINT "WELCOME TO COMPUTER CHALLENGE. THIS PROGRAM CON-
      TAINS COMPUTER ACTIVITIES THAT REQUIRE ONLY A BASIC KNOWL-
      EDGE OF PROGRAMMING."
20    PRINT "DO YOU WISH TO PLAY? TYPE IN YES OR NO."
30    INPUT A$
40    IF A$ = "NO" GOTO 10
50    PRINT "PLEASE SELECT ONE OF THE ACTIVITIES THAT FOLLOW: (A)
      CREATE A WORD SEARCH PROGRAM THAT CONTAINS WELL-KNOWN
      MYTHOLOGICAL HEROES. (B) USING COMPUTER GRAPHICS, CREATE A
      GREEK OR ROMAN SYMBOL. (C) DEVELOP A PROGRAM THAT STORES
      THE NAMES OF THE PRINCIPAL MEMBERS OF THE GREEK AND ROMAN
      PANTHEONS, IDENTIFIES THEIR SYMBOLS, AND DESCRIBES THEIR
      SPHERES OF RESPONSIBILITY. THE USER SHOULD BE ABLE TO TYPE IN
      THE NAME OF A GOD OR GODDESS AND RECEIVE THE CORRESPOND-
      ING INFORMATION."
60    INPUT B$
70    PRINT "I HAVE CHOSEN TO" B$
80    PRINT "GOOD LUCK!"
90    GOTO 10
```

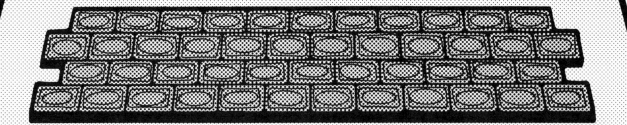

Name_____

Get in the Act!

Choose and do at least one of the activities described below.

Make a Lasting Impression

Using soap, sugar cubes, wooden blocks, or other inexpensive materials, build a model of a Greek amphitheater.

Working in papier-mâché or some other medium with which you are familiar, create a mask for a traditional Greek character.

Draw up a playbill for a well-known Greek play.

Illustrate a scene from a Greek drama of your choice.

Sketch several typical Greek costumes.

Produce a Written Masterpiece

Be a theater critic. Write a newspaper column in which you critique a Greek play.

Write a script for a Greek comedy set in modern times.

Draw up a casting list for a Greek tragedy. On this list, name all of the characters and describe in detail the demands of each role.

Stage a Production

Write the script for a television show in which you interview the characters in a Greek play.

Prepare and present a choral reading of a Greek myth.

Dramatize a Greek myth as children's theater.

Tape record the first scene of a well-known Greek play—complete with sound effects.

Mythical Mirth

Bring smiles to the faces of those around you with a little mythical mirth. On a separate sheet of paper, write some definitions, jokes, and riddles with a mythical twist. Follow the examples given below.

Riddles

Question: How did the ancient Greeks know that Prometheus was excited?

Answer: They saw that he was all fired up!

Daffy Definitions

Question: What do you call Hera when she is jealous?

Answer: A green goddess or a green queen.

Knock Knock Jokes

"Knock, knock."
"Who's there?"
"Demeter."
"Demeter who?"
"Demeter's running on the taxicab that's waiting outside."

Tom Swifties

"You're sure to fall in love now," said Cupid sharply.

"Last one into the cave is a rotten egg," said Odysseus adventurously.

"You'll never get out of this cave alive," shrieked Polyphemus blindly.

Just Plain Pediment

The triangular section above the columns on the front of each Greek temple is called a **pediment**. In ancient times, pediments were usually ornamented with sculpture. These sculptures often depicted gods and goddesses, heroes and heroines in battles, athletic contests, or moments of quiet thought.

The pediment pictured below is much too plain. Create an appropriate design for it.

Mything in Action

Choose and do one of the activities described below. When you finish, share what you have created with the class.

Many rules of personal and social behavior are evident in Greek myths. Write a book of etiquette or a code of law based on your knowledge of Greek myths.

Write an essay in which you name a myth you would like to be in, describe the part you would play, and tell the reasons for your choice.

Create a word search or a crossword puzzle based on one of the myths you have read.

Across

1. The fruit Persephone ate in the lower world
3. Demeter's daughter
5. The name given Demeter by the Romans
6. Demeter's mother

Down

2. Greek goddess of the earth's fruits, especially corn
4. Greek god of the lower world

	¹P	O	M	E	G	R	A	N	A	T	E
		²D									
	³P	E	R	S	E	P	⁴H	O	N	E	
		M					A				
		E					D				
		T				⁵C	E	R	E	S	
		E					S				
		⁶R	H	E	A						

Create a Card

The gods and goddesses on Mount Olympus have fallen on hard times and have been forced to go into business for themselves. Based on what you know, match their qualifications and experience with the services listed here. Then, create business cards for some of them. On these cards include the name of the deity, name of the business, address, logo, and appropriate slogan.

- beauty salon

- delivery service

- electrical supplies

- florist

- hunting supplies

- jewelry and crafts

- pet shop

- seafood merchant

- undertaker

ECHO STEREO
ECHO STEREO
WHERE TWICE THE SOUND IS ALWAYS FOUND
WHERE TWICE THE SOUND IS ALWAYS FOUND
2420 DEEP CAVERN DRIVE
2420 DEEP CAVERN DRIVE
HOLLOW HILLS
HOLLOW HILLS

Write a Résumé

The gods and goddesses on Mount Olympus have fallen on hard times and have been forced to find ways of earning money. Some of them have gone into business for themselves, but others are still looking for employment.

Choose a god or goddess. On a separate sheet of paper, write a résumé this particular deity might use to get a job. Remember to include an address and brief descriptions of any education and training, professional experience, special interests, and unusual talents or natural abilities. If myths don't provide all of the information you need to complete the résumé, use your imagination.

PERSEPHONE	**PROFESSIONAL RÉSUMÉ**
Summer Address:	c/o Ceres 15 Grain Road Mount Olympus
Winter Address:	c/o Hades in the Lower World
EDUCATION	Received a diploma from Mount Olympus High School.
WORK EXPERIENCE	Flower Gatherer on the Nysian Plain for Pantheon Posies, a small and very exclusive florist shop.
HOBBIES AND SPECIAL INTERESTS	Enjoys gardening and growing things.

It's a Real Zoo!

Chimera

Pegasus

Harpy

Unicorn

The gods and goddesses on Mount Olympus have asked you to design some enclosures to house their monster menagerie. Create a zoo for these mythological creatures. Remember that some of them are difficult to restrain and may be dangerous. Give careful thought to their individual characteristics and needs so that you can create appropriate settings that will enable them to be comfortably contained and safely viewed.

Centaur

Minotaur

Fashion a Finish

Below is a well-known fable. After you have read it, fashion a finish of your own. On a separate sheet of paper, rewrite this fable with a new ending and moral.

Belling the Cat

The mice in the old house were worried. Every night, when they went in search of food, their numbers were reduced by a large, gray cat who was partial to mouse meat. As the mice saw it, they were faced with a choice between starving to death and being eaten.

Finally, the desperate survivors met in the safety of a mouse hole to devise a plan. They had talked fruitlessly for some time when suddenly a young mouse jumped up and said, "I have the perfect plan! We'll fasten a bell to the cat's tail. Then, when he walks, the bell will ring. We'll hear the bell, know that the cat's approaching, and be able to hide." The young mouse sat down, delighted with his cleverness, and enjoyed the applause of his fellow mice.

Then a wise and wizened mouse stood up to speak. "Youngster," he said, "your plan is an excellent one. I have only one question—who is to tie the bell on the cat's tail?" Not one of the mice responded.

Moral: Don't offer plans if you're not prepared to carry them out.

Heraclean Hurdles

It was only through strength and cunning that Heracles was able to take in stride the twelve labors devised for him by Eurystheus.

Can you imagine the labors that might be planned by

- an archaeologist,
- an astronomer,
- a computer program designer,
- an environmentalist,
- a science fiction fan,
- a sports coach, or
- a United Nations agency?

Select one of these individuals or groups. On the lines below, list and describe twelve labors this planner might devise. If you need additional space, use a separate sheet of paper.

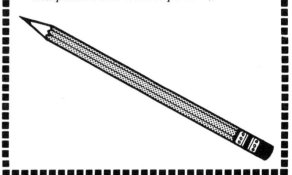

Twelve Labors Created by an Environmentalist

1. *Clean up a recent coastal oil spill.*
2. *Depollute the Great Lakes.*
3. *Remove excess hydrocarbons from the air to prevent the greenhouse effect.*
4. *Find a safe, efficient, nonpolluting source of inexpensive and reliable power.*

Twelve Labors Created by a/an _____

_____

_____

_____

_____

_____

_____

_____

_____

_____

_____

_____

Myth Match

As a part of the Greek mythic tradition, each god and goddess in the pantheon had **attributes**, objects that were sacred to or closely associated with the deity and that, in some instances, even came to symbolize his or her power or person.

Match these Olympians with their attributes by writing the correct letter on each line. If you are uncertain about one of these myth matches, look up the deity in a classical dictionary, encyclopedia, or book about mythology. Another source of information might be art books in which statues and other representations of these gods and goddesses are pictured.

Olympians	Attributes
_____ 1. Aphrodite	**a.** staff (caduceus), tortoise, wide-brimmed traveling hat, and winged sandals
_____ 2. Apollo	**b.** bear, bow, and moon
_____ 3. Athena	**c.** peacock
_____ 4. Ares	**d.** vulture
_____ 5. Artemis	**e.** laurel tree, cow, and dolphin
_____ 6. Hades	**f.** apple, myrtle, rose, dove, sparrow, swallow, and swan
_____ 7. Hera	**g.** eagle, scepter, thunderbolt, and oak tree
_____ 8. Hermes	**h.** olive tree and owl
_____ 9. Poseidon	**i.** bull, dolphin, horse, and trident
_____ 10. Zeus	**j.** black stallion, helmet, and staff

Name_____

Mythrepresentation

The Greeks often honored their deities by picturing them on coins and vases and sculpting statues to represent them. First, select a god or goddess. Then, either produce a patch or cast a coin (in mint condition, of course) to commemorate this deity. For ideas, refer to the list of deities and their roles on pages 18–20 or to the list of attributes on page 92.

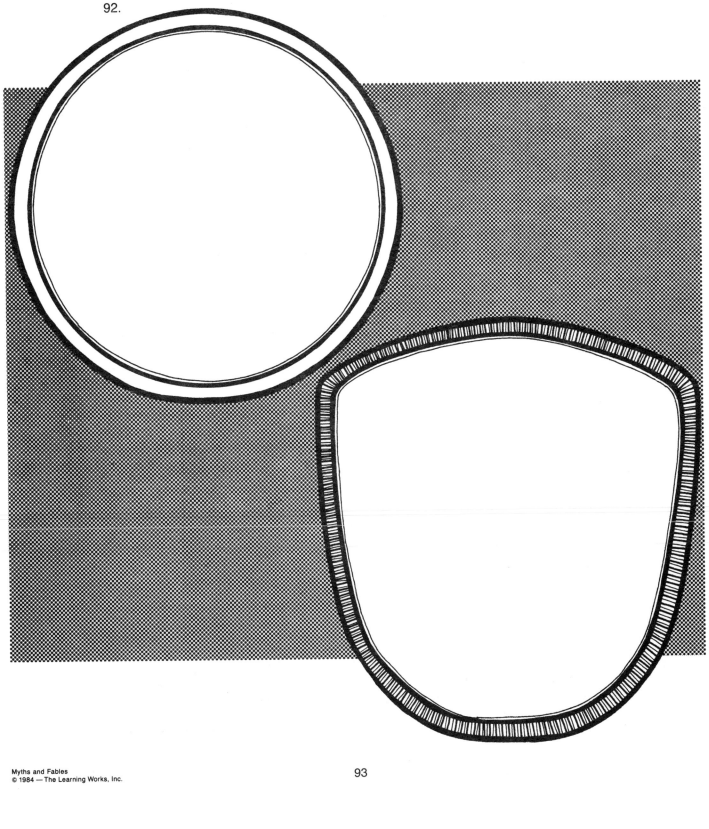

Debatable Proverbs

A rolling stone gathers no moss. **A**	A rolling stone gathers no moss **P**
Too many cooks spoil the broth. **A**	Too many cooks spoil the broth. **P**
He who hesitates is lost. **A**	He who hesitates is lost. **P**
Haste makes waste. **A**	Haste makes waste. **P**
The early bird catches the worm. **A**	The early bird catches the worm. **P**
Look before you leap. **A**	Look before you leap. **P**
Slow and steady wins the race. **A**	Slow and steady wins the race. **P**
A bird in the hand is worth two in the bush. **A**	A bird in the hand is worth two in the bush. **P**
A stitch in time saves nine. **A**	A stitch in time saves nine. **P**
Don't count your chickens before they're hatched. **A**	Don't count your chickens before they're hatched. **P**

Name_____

Hands On

Using some of these tools and materials,

brushes
cardboard
clay
cloth
crayons
felt
flour
foil
glue
metal
paint
paper
papier-mâché
pencils
scissors
soap
string
tape
wood
yarn

just

build
carve
draw
engineer
fold
knit
paint
paste
sculpt
sew

one of these items—

Athena's shield
a geometric design
a Greek temple
a model of Mount Olympus
a model of Odysseus's ship
a model of the Trojan horse
a small hang glider for Icarus
a statue of Pygmalion
winged sandals

to become part of a classroom display.

An Ancient Arboretum

How many plants can you pluck from the pages of mythology for your own modern Greek garden? Consider each of the following categories:

flowers

narcissus

rose

_____

_____

_____

ground covers

moss

_____

_____

_____

_____

fruits

apple

pomegranate

_____

_____

trees

laurel

oak

olive

willow

_____

grains

wheat

_____

_____

_____

_____

vegetables

corn

_____

_____

_____

_____

- First, list your choices by category on the lines above.

- Then, on a separate sheet of paper, create an original landscape design that includes some of your favorites.

It's Monstrous

Mix and match to make a monster. Simply fill in the blanks to give it

1. the head of a _____
   _____

2. the body of a _____
   _____

3. the tail of a _____
   _____

4. the eyes of a _____
   _____

5. the ears of a _____
   _____

6. the horns of a _____
   _____

7. the mouth of a _____
   _____

8. the forelegs of a _____
   _____

9. the hind legs of a _____
   _____

10. the feet of a _____
    _____

11. the wings of a _____
    _____

Once you have described your monster, depict it by

- drawing a picture
- gluing a collage
- making a costume or mask
- sculpting a model
- sewing a puppet

Letter Language

An **alphabet** is a system of letters used to represent the different sounds in a language. The word **alphabet** is made up of two Greek words, *alpha* and *beta*, the first two letters of the Greek alphabet. The Greeks adopted the Phoenician alphabet and added vowels to it, thus making twenty-four letters. Shortly thereafter, the Romans borrowed the Greek alphabet and changed it into the Roman capital letters used in the English alphabet today.

But the Greek alphabet did not vanish: it is still in use. Not only is it used in Greece, but Greek letters are used throughout the world in special contexts. For example, they are used to stand for the names of honorary, professional, and social fraternities, sororities, and societies. These letters are also used in certain scientific writings and mathematical formulas.

1 Using the chart found under the heading *alphabet* in a dictionary or encyclopedia, compare the appearances of one letter in several different alphabets (for example, Arabic, Greek, Hebrew, and Russian) or trace the evolution of one letter from Phoenician through Greek and Roman to English. In what ways has the letter changed? In what ways is it still the same?

2 Look for Greek letters in advertisements and textbooks, on sweatshirts and the rear windows of automobiles, and elsewhere. Make a list of the ones you find. On this list, write the letter or letters, tell what they mean or stand for, and then describe where you found them.

3 Use the letters of the Greek alphabet to create a code to share with a friend. Because the English alphabet has twenty-six letters while the Greek alphabet has only twenty-four and because the Greek alphabet does not have direct equivalents for some of the letters found in the English alphabet, you will need to use your imagination.

THE GREEK ALPHABET

Α	α	**alpha**
Β	β	**beta**
Γ	γ	**gamma**
Δ	δ	**delta**
Ε	ε	**epsilon**
Ζ	ζ	**zeta**
Η	η	**eta**
Θ	θ	**theta**
Ι	ι	**iota**
Κ	κ	**kappa**
Λ	λ	**lambda**
Μ	μ	**mu**
Ν	ν	**nu**
Ξ	ξ	**xi**
Ο	ο	**omicron**
Π	π	**pi**
Ρ	ρ	**rho**
Σ	σ	**sigma**
Τ	τ	**tau**
Υ	υ	**upsilon**
Φ	φ	**phi**
Χ	χ	**chi**
Ψ	ψ	**psi**
Ω	ω	**omega**

Stellar Creations

A **constellation** is an arbitrary grouping, or configuration, of stars. Currently, there are eighty-eight recognized constellations. Many of them take their names from Greek mythology. For example, there are constellations named **Hydra, Pegasus,** and **Perseus.**

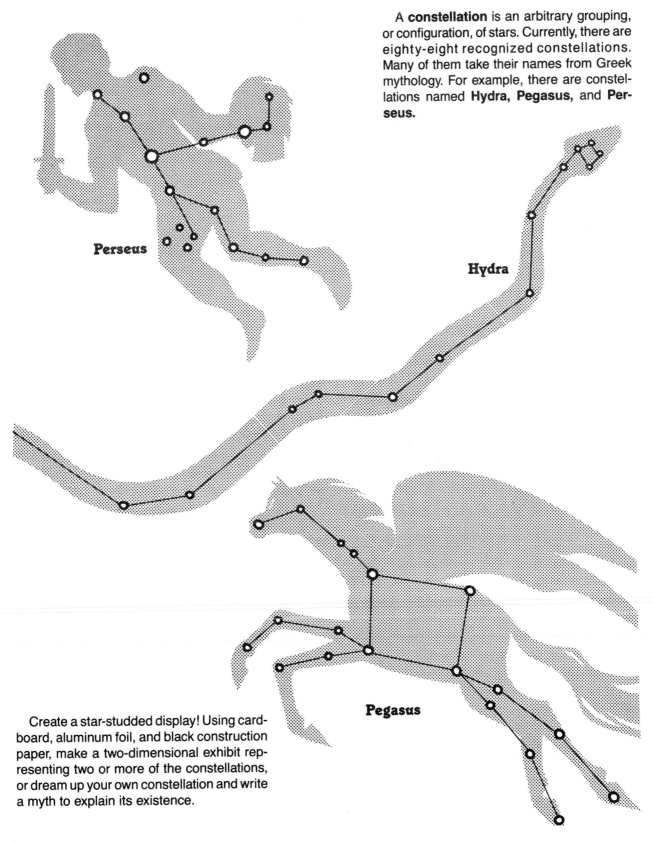

Create a star-studded display! Using cardboard, aluminum foil, and black construction paper, make a two-dimensional exhibit representing two or more of the constellations, or dream up your own constellation and write a myth to explain its existence.

Time Out

JANUS

It is for **Janus,** the god of beginnings and endings, that **January,** the month that ends the old year and begins each new one, is named. How or for whom were the other months named?

January ____*named for Janus*____

February _____

March _____

April _____

May _____

June _____

July _____

August _____

September _____

October _____

November _____

December _____

Explore the resources available to you. When and by whom was our present calendar devised? How and for whom were the days of the week named?

_____

_____

_____

_____

Sunday _____

Monday _____

Tuesday _____

Wednesday _____

Thursday _____

Friday _____

Saturday _____

- Create a calendar based on mythology.
- Design and build a functional sundial.

Name_____

An Olympian Election

It's election time on Mount Olympus and time for you to do a little politicking of your own.

ZAP 'EM WITH ZEUS

GET IN THE SWIM POSEIDON FOR PRESIDENT

DEMETER? YOU CAN'T BEAT HER! SECRETARY OF AGRICULTURE

A VOTE FOR APOLLO IS A BRIGHT IDEA!

BE WARY OF ARES DEPARTMENT OF DEFENSE

☐ Think of names for two Olympian political parties.

☐ Create a symbol and write a brief platform for each one.

☐ Poll the gods and goddesses regarding their political preferences.

☐ Register each deity as a member of one of the recognized political parties.

☐ Invent and describe the duties of some elective offices that need to be filled.

☐ Select candidates from among the deities to run for these offices.

☐ Prepare banners, buttons, and/or placards to advertise their candidacy.

☐ Write a speech one candidate might use to win the election.

☐ Tape record your speech and make it a real winner!

An Olympic Challenge

The Olympic Games include some unusual composite contests in which participants must compete in several separate events. Among these composite contests are the **biathlon,** which is a winter contest that includes two events, cross-country skiing and rifle shooting; the **pentathlon,** which consists of five events; and the **decathlon,** which includes ten events: the 110-meter high hurdles, the javelin and discus throws, the shot put, the pole vault, the high jump, the long jump, and 100-meter, 400-meter, and 1,500-meter runs.

Ideas for new composite contests arrive at the International Olympic Headquarters frequently, and yours could be among them. Get the jump on the competition by creating an Olympic challenge of your own.

1. Decide whether your composite contest will be a part of the Summer or Winter Olympics.

2. Select and list the separate events that your composite contest will include.

3. Write a description of your composite contest.

4. Write specific rules for your composite contest.

5. Establish a point system for officials to use in scoring your contest.

6. Name your contest.

7. Write a memo to the International Olympic Committee describing your Olympic challenge in detail.

MEMO

To: International Olympic Committee
From: Sherri Butterfield
Re: New Olympic Challenge
Date: August 10

For your consideration, I am proposing a new composite contest to be called the Cliff Climb with Rappel and to be included in the Summer Olympic Games. This contest would consist of a series of sheer face climbs and include at least one rappel. It would test the strength, stamina, and judgment of entrants; and performance would be evaluated on the basis of both time and form.

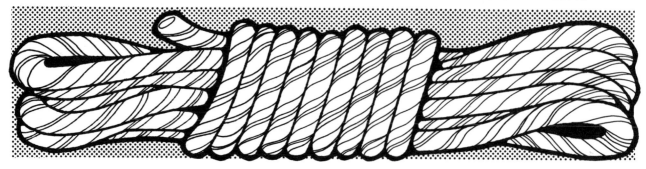

Chariot Chatter

Today, many people use bumper stickers as one way of expressing their thoughts and feelings about everything from pets to politics. As far as we know, this custom is a modern one that did not exist in ancient Greece; but it can be amusing to imagine what sentiments specific Greeks would have selected, had they had the opportunity. For example, Icarus might have chosen "Flying is for the birds" or "I'd rather be sailing."

On a separate sheet of paper, create bumper stickers for the chariots of the gods and other characters and creatures from Greek mythology. Let your imagination run wild. If you need inspiration, think about some of the sentiments you have seen on car bumpers recently and match them to characters you've read about.

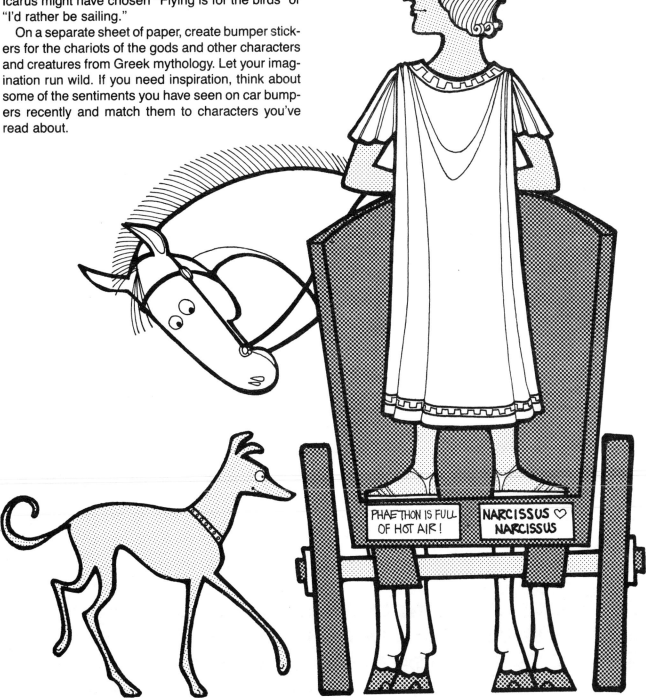

PHAETHON IS FULL OF HOT AIR!

NARCISSUS ♡ NARCISSUS

It's Toga Time

Use this simple checklist to plan a party with a Greek or Roman theme.

☐ Set the time, place, and theme for your party.

☐ Choose and describe the appropriate costume or dress.

☐ Decide how many guests you want to invite and list their names.

☐ Have the time, place, theme, dress, and guest list approved by the adult in charge.

☐ Plan the menu. Include at least some foods that the Greeks or Romans enjoyed.

☐ Design and create the invitations.

☐ Select games to be played at the party.

☐ Plan and make arrangements for any additional entertainment you want.

☐ Decide what prizes will be given to game winners.

☐ Decide what awards will be presented for the best costumes.

☐ Decide how you will decorate to create the mood you want.

☐ Three weeks before the party, address and send invitations to the names on your guest list. Be sure to indicate on the invitations if you want guests to let you know whether or not they are planning to come.

☐ List the paper goods (plates, cups, and napkins), prizes, awards, and decorating materials you will need and purchase them.

☐ List the food and other grocery items you will need and purchase them.

☐ Prepare the food.

☐ Clean and decorate the place.

☐ Enjoy the party.

☐ Clean up after the party so that you leave the place *exactly* as you found it.

YOU ARE INVITED TO A GRAND GATHERING OF THE GREEK GODS AND GODDESSES. DON'T MYTH IT!

Name _____

Mythical Menus

In the spaces provided, create a sign for a restaurant located near Mount Olympus. Then hand letter and illustrate a menu of heavenly delicacies designed to delight the Olympian diners who frequent this establishment. Consider including such palate pleasers as chilled eye of newt, meat Promethean, corn (in season), ambrosia supreme, and nectar.

Menu

An A-Mazing Accomplishment

Minos, a son of Zeus and the king of Crete, had a monster that was half man and half bull. The king kept this Minotaur, as the monster was called, in an enclosure designed by Daedalus. This enclosure, known as the Labyrinth, was a maze so intricate that the monster could not escape.

Now King Minos had a son named Androgeos, who was a very gifted athlete. When Androgeos entered and won all of the games of the Panathenaea, some of the other athletes were jealous of his abilities and killed him. To avenge the murder of his son, Minos made war on the Athenians and forced them to send to Crete every year seven youths and seven maidens as a tribute. These unfortunate young people were compelled to enter the Labyrinth, where they wandered helplessly until, one by one, they encountered the Minotaur and were devoured by it.

Only the legendary hero Theseus was able to enter the maze and to return alive. On the advice of Ariadne, Minos's daughter, he carried a spool of thread, which he unwound as he went. Theseus found and killed the Minotaur and then followed the thread back through the Labyrinth to its exit.

Use a pencil to wind your way through the maze below. Then engineer your own labyrinth to contain a secret or perplex a friend. Be sure to include many false turns and dead ends.

The Athens Connection

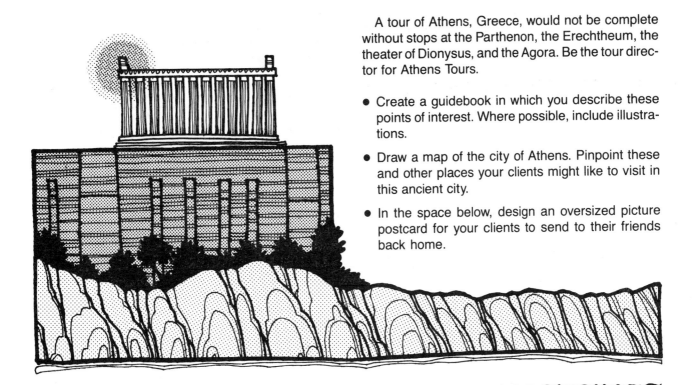

A tour of Athens, Greece, would not be complete without stops at the Parthenon, the Erechtheum, the theater of Dionysus, and the Agora. Be the tour director for Athens Tours.

- Create a guidebook in which you describe these points of interest. Where possible, include illustrations.

- Draw a map of the city of Athens. Pinpoint these and other places your clients might like to visit in this ancient city.

- In the space below, design an oversized picture postcard for your clients to send to their friends back home.

Reading Skills Checklist

List students' last names on the lines at the left. When a skill is introduced, draw a diagonal line through the corresponding box and shade the upper portion. When that same skill is mastered, shade the remaining portion of the box.

Names	Vocabulary											Literal Comprehension							Interpretive Comprehension				Literary Terms											
	Analogies	Antonyms	Connotation/Denotation	Context Clues	Dictionary Skills	Homonyms	Multiple Meanings	Prefixes	Suffixes	Synonyms	Thesaurus	Compare and Contrast	Fact or Opinion	Locating Information	Main Idea	Recognizing Author's Purpose	Sequencing	Supporting Details	Cause and Effect	Drawing Conclusions	Making Inferences	Point of View	Antagonist/Protagonist	Characterization	Climax	Conflict	Figurative Language	Flashback	Foreshadowing	Mood	Plot	Setting	Symbol	Theme	Tone

Bibliography

Aeschylus One: Oresteia, Agamemon, the Libation Bearers, the Eumenides. Translated by Richmond Lattimore. Chicago, Ill.: University of Chicago Press, 1953.

Aeschylus Two; Four Tragedies: Prometheus Bound, Seven Against Thebes, the Persians, the Suppliant Maidens. Edited by David Grene and Richmond Lattimore. Chicago, Ill.: University of Chicago Press, 1956.

Aesop's Fables. Edited by Anne T. White. New York: Random House, 1964.

Asimov, Isaac. *Words from the Myths.* New York: New American Library, 1969.

Benson, Sally. *Stories of the Gods and Heroes.* New York: Dell, 1979.

Berens, E. M. *Myths and Legends of Ancient Greece and Rome.* Dover, N.H.: Longwood, 1977.

Carpenter, Thomas H., and Robert J. Gula. *Mythology: Greek and Roman.* Wellesley Hills, Mass.: Independent School Press, 1977.

Coolidge, Olivia. *Greek Myths.* Boston, Mass.: Houghton Mifflin, 1949.

Coolidge, Olivia. *Hercules and Other Tales from Greek Myths.* New York: Scholastic, n.d.

Coolidge, Olivia. *The Trojan War.* Boston, Mass.: Houghton Mifflin, 1952.

D'Aulaire, Ingri, and Edgar P. D'Aulaire. *D'Aulaire Book of Greek Myths.* New York: Doubleday, 1982.

Euripides Three: Four Tragedies. Edited by David Grene and Richmond Lattimore. Chicago, Ill.: University of Chicago Press, 1958.

Evslin, Bernard. *The Adventures of Ulysses.* New York: Bantam, 1978.

Evslin, Bernard, Dorothy Evslin, and Ned Hooper. *Heroes and Monsters of Greek Myths.* New York: Scholastic, 1970.

Frazer, Sir James G. *The Golden Bough.* Abridged ed. New York: Macmillan, 1967.

Gates, Doris. *The Golden God: Apollo.* Greek Myths Series. New York: Penguin Books, 1983.

Gates, Doris. *Lord of the Sky: Zeus.* Greek Myths Series. New York: Penguin Books, 1982.

Gates, Doris. *Mightiest of Mortals: Heracles.* Greek Myths Series. New York: Viking Press, 1975.

Gayley, Charles M. *The Classic Myths in English Literature and Art.* Dover, N.H.: Longwood, 1977.

Graves, Robert. *Greek Myths.* New York: Doubleday, 1982.

Grene, David, and Richmond Lattimore, eds. *The Complete Greek Tragedies.* 4 vols. Chicago, Ill.: University of Chicago Press, 1942–1960.

Hamilton, Edith. *The Greek Way.* New York: W. W. Norton, 1983.

Hamilton, Edith. *Mythology.* New York: New American Library, 1971.

Handford, S. A., trans. *Fables of Aesop.* Classics Series. New York: Penguin Books, 1964.

Kottmeyer, William A., et al. *Greek and Roman Myths.* New York: McGraw-Hill, 1962.

McLean, Mollie, and Anne Wiseman. *The Adventures of Greek Heroes.* Boston, Mass.: Houghton Mifflin, 1972.

Moffitt, Frederick J. *Tales from Ancient Greece.* The World Folktale Library. Morristown, N.J.: Silver Burdett, 1979.

Rees, Ennis. *Fables from Aesop.* New York: Oxford University Press, 1966.

Sophocles One. Edited by David Grene and Richmond Lattimore. Complete Greek Tragedies Series. Chicago, Ill.: University of Chicago Press, 1954.

Sophocles Two. Edited by David Grene and Richmond Lattimore. Complete Greek Tragedies Series. Chicago, Ill.: University of Chicago Press, 1957.

Warrington, John. *Everyman's Classical Dictionary.* 3rd rev. ed. Everyman's Reference Library. Totowa, N.J.: Biblio Distribution Centre, 1978.

Answer Key

Pages 7-9, Pretest
1-14. Answers will vary, depending on the myth each student uses.
15. forecast *or* prediction
16. alarm, dread, fear, fright, horror, *or* terror
17. a small and subordinate part of a larger group, particularly a military group
18. against
19. able to be
20. contrast

Page 11, Align in Time
a. 12
b. 1
c. 10
d. 11
e. 3
f. 9
g. 8
h. 5
i. 7
j. 4
k. 6
l. 2

Time line for page 11

A.D. 500 — a
A.D. 250
0 — d, c
— f
250 B.C. — g
500 B.C. — i
750 B.C. — K, h, j
1000 B.C.
1250 B.C.
1500 B.C. — e, l
1750 B.C.
2000 B.C. — b

Page 12, An Olympic Challenge
Answers will vary but might include the following observations:
Similarities
1. Both posters advertise the Olympics.
2. Both posters invite readers to witness, cheer, marvel, and applaud.
3. Both posters list artistic and cultural events as part of the larger Olympic celebration.
4. Both posters mention an event called the pentathlon.
5. Both posters mention races as being among the Olympic events.
Differences
1. The posters are set in different typefaces.
2. One poster advertises the LXXXIInd ancient Olympiad, while the other advertises the XXIIIrd modern Olympiad.
3. One poster tells of competition among men, while the other tells of competition among men and women.
4. The poster for the ancient Olympics mentions the pancratium; the poster for the modern Olympics does not mention this event.
5. One poster tells of competitors from Greek city-states; the other tells of competitors from countries throughout the world.

Page 17, Outline Odyssey
A.
1. Lightning was transformed into bolts hurled by Zeus.
2. Echoes were the moans of lovesick maidens.
3. The sun was a luminous chariot driven by Helios.
B.
1. They built temples to honor the deities described in myths.
2. The temple to Apollo at Delphi is well known.
3. The temple to Athena is perhaps the most famous in the world.
C.
1. The gods argued and fought.
2. The goddesses became jealous.
3. Both gods and goddesses were vulnerable.

D.
1. Details were added.
2. Exploits were exaggerated.
3. Heroes battled incredible monsters.
E.
1. When the Romans conquered the Greeks, Latinized versions of Greek myths survived.
2. After the destruction of the Roman Empire, Greek and Roman myths continued to be enjoyed.
3. Both children and adults enjoy myths today.

Pages 18-20, The Pantheon—A Family Affair
Drawings of family trees may vary somewhat, depending upon the sources from which pertinent information is obtained.

Pages 21-22, Chaotic Creation
The correct order by letter should be as follows: C, L, Q, S, H, E, N, R, J (*or* J, R), I, T, P, A, O, M, G, D, F, K, B (*or* B, K)

Page 24, Celestial Symbols
1. *Symbol:* caduceus
   Association: symbolic staff of the messenger god Hermes
   Modern Use: symbol of physicians and of the medical profession
2. *Symbol:* Hermes *or* Mercury
   Association: messenger of the gods
   Modern Use: symbol of Florists Telegraph (*or* Transworld) delivery (FTD)
3. *Symbol:* eagle (with an oak or olive branch and arrows or thunderbolts)
   Association: symbol and attributes of Zeus
   Modern Use: symbol of the United States of America and of the presidency of that country
4. *Symbol:* winged sandal
   Association: worn by Hermes to make him fleet of foot and able to fly
   Modern use: symbol of Goodyear Tire and Rubber Company
5. *Symbol:* winged horse Pegasus
   Association: symbol of strength, speed, endurance, and victory
   Modern Use: symbol of *Reader's Digest* and of Mobil Oil Company and its affiliated service stations

Pages 25-26, Olympian Verse-ality Cards
The match-ups should be as follows:
1. F
2. E
3. D
4. C
5. B
6. A
7. H
8. G
9. L
10. K
11. J
12. I

Page 33, How's That Again?
Answers will vary but might include the following observations:
Similarities
1. Both the mythological account and the scientific one attempt to explain the sound phenomenon known as an echo.
2. Both accounts describe an echo as returning or repeating sounds.

Answer Key
(continued)

Page 33, How's That Again? (continued)

Differences

1. The myth says that the mimicking sound we call an echo is all that remains of a wood nymph named Echo; while the scientific explanation says that, when sound waves strike smooth, hard surfaces, they sometimes bounce back so that the sound they carry is heard again.
2. There are characters (Zeus, a young woman, Hera, Echo, and Narcissus) in the myth, but there are no characters in the scientific explanation.

Page 35, Olympian Analogies

1. Uranus
2. Mars
3. Helios
4. appearance
5. marathon
6. temper
7. Promethean
8. ignominy
9. television
10. omnipotent
11. arachnid
12. trident
13. attribute
14. titan
15. narrator

Pages 38-39, Special Effects

1. Because Phaethon boasted often of his lineage, his playmates demanded proof that he was, indeed, the son of Helios, god of the sun.
2. Because Phaethon grew weary of being teased by his playmates, he decided to visit his father, Helios.
3. Because Helios was touched by the boy's plight, he reluctantly agreed to let him drive the chariot of the sun.
4. Because Phaethon was young and inexperienced, he could not control the horses that pulled the chariot.
5. Because the chariot of the sun came so near the earth, the sun's heat caused mountains (*or* volcanoes) to explode.
6. Because the chariot of the sun came so near the earth, the sun's heat turned lush, grassy plains into parched deserts.
7. Because Phaethon was struck by Zeus's thunderbolt, he fell to earth.
8. Because Phaethon's mother and sisters grieved continually for him, the gods transformed them into willow trees so that they could stand, weeping near his grave, forever.

Page 40-41, An Amazing Quest

1. Persians
2. Promethean
3. Pan
4. west wind
5. morphine
6. finger
7. hypocrite
8. a musical instrument that resembles an organ
9. the waters of a lake that surrounded him and receded when he tried to drink from them
10. above, beyond, over, *or* super
11. Muse
12. top (*or* head)
13. No
    The Greek stadium was a course for footraces.
14. seats on both sides
    circular
    oval
15. He spoke for the gods, gave wise advice, and sometimes predicted the outcome of such future events as battles and quests.
    one who speaks for a deity
    prophet *or* seer
16. a right triangle
    Pythagoras
17. Yes
    Hermetic means "airtight, impervious to outside influences."
18. The chorus comments in unison on the situation or action.
19. having great magnitude, force, or power

Page 49, Thesaurus Therapy

1. crowded
2. lived
3. problem
4. rough
5. people
6. good
7. happy
8. life
9. kindness
10. tell not to
11. yelled
12. amazed *or* surprised
13. abrupt, blunt, brief *or* gruff
14. tempting
15. smell
16. unwilling
17. painful punishment

Pages 45-46, A Case of Mythtaken Identity

Personality Trait	Method of Characterization	Textual Evidence
cleverness	what the character does	"As Prometheus was leaving, he threw some raw meat onto the fire."
vanity	what the author says about the character	"Pleased with himself for thinking of an answer to their dilemma, Prometheus searched throughout Olympus until he found Zeus."
narrowmindedness	what another character says about the character	"'Prometheus, you fail to see the whole picture. . . . I forbid you to give it to them!' bellowed Zeus."
rebelliousness	what the character says	"'I'll not take no for an answer,' he muttered."

Suitor B is the real Prometheus.
Underlined statements and passages may vary, but should agree with the fact that the real Prometheus is headstrong, impulsive, and inclined to act rather than to wait and see.

****

Answer Key
(continued)

Page 50, Keep an Eye on the Future
1. Hera was known, both on Olympus and on the earth, for her incredible jealousy. ... Zeus soon learned that he must protect those with whom he spoke, and he became very cautious, always watching for the approach of his wife. Yet even Zeus could not anticipate her appearance, for Hera was cunning.
2. If Zeus and Io had heeded this warning, they would not have met at all or they would have met in disguise so that Hera could not recognize them and would not become jealous.
3. Answers will vary.

Page 55, Pygmalion and Galatea
1. He was a talented sculptor.
2. He created a marble statue of a beautiful maiden.
3. He fell in love with it.
4. It came to life.

Page 56, Undercover Themes
Answers will vary but might include the following responses:
1. The ideal can be approached but never attained.
2. Love is a relationship that must be built over time and cannot be created in an instant *or,* in the words of Oscar Wilde, "When the gods wish to punish us, they answer our prayers."
3. The ideal can be achieved in art but not in life *or* the ideal and the real are incompatible.
4. Vain hopes are often shattered like the dreams of those who wake.
5. Art imitates life.
6. Mortals should not try to imitate the gods in either appearance or achievement.

Page 60, Be a Synonym Seer
Across	Down
1. narcissistic	2. cloth
5. pedagogue	3. titanic
6. laurels	4. ceramics
8. echo	7. labyrinth
10. panic	9. Olympian

Page 65, A Mythinterpretation
1. ruthless – unkind
2. obstinacy – determination
3. rash – hasty
4. submissive – obedient
5. ferret out – search for
6. voraciously – eagerly
7. interminable – perpetual
8. hacked – cut
9. vain – proud
10. vagabond – wanderer

Page 66, A Heroic Leap in Time
1. Heracles' infancy, when he strangled two serpents easily
2. Heracles' youth, when he was instructed in chariot driving, wrestling, fighting in heavy armor, singing, and playing the lyre
3. Heracles' coming of age and marrying Megara
4. The birth of Heracles' children
5. Heracles' murdering his own children
6. Heracles' visit to the oracle

7. Heracles' arriving to do penance in the court of King Eurystheus
8. The first labor—killing the Nemean lion
9. The second labor—killing the Lernean hydra
10. The third labor—capturing the Arcadian stag
11. The fourth labor—destroying the Erymanthian boar

Page 67, Ferret out the Facts
1. F	6. O	11. O
2. F	7. F	12. O
3. O	8. F	13. F
4. F	9. O	14. O
5. F	10. F	15. F

Page 77, Fable Figures
1. the prince and a jaguar
2. a man's eyesight and that of a hawk
3. a mother's hug and that of a koala
4-10. Answers will vary.

Page 79, Concrete Conclusions
Answers will vary but might include the following responses:
1. It is big and slow.
2. It is a relatively slow bicycle race or a race for novice riders.
3. She is a fancy dresser and takes great pride in her appearance.
4. It is slow and steady.
5. He climbs around a lot and is very adventuresome.
6. It is brightly colored and may have a bold pattern.
7. He is quick or he hops from patient to patient.
8. It is showing signs of strength and is marked by rising prices.

Pages 80-81, Posttest
1. W	9. S	17. D
2. I	10. T	18. G
3. C	11. L	19. B
4. U	12. Q	20. H
5. V	13. F	21. O
6. E	14. J	22. A
7. P	15. K	23. X
8. N	16. R	24. M

25. to inform (*or* to explain)
26. to entertain
27. We now have scientific explanations for many of the puzzling natural phenomena that were once explained only by myths. We do not need myths to inform (*or* explain) so we use them to entertain (*or* amuse).
28. astronaut
29. repeat
30. conceited
31. far off; distant; remote
32. unattractive (Its connotation is "hideous" or "repulsive.")
33. thesaurus
34. opinion
35. fact

Page 92, Myth Match
1. f	4. d	7. c	10. g
2. e	5. b	8. a	
3. h	6. j	9. i	

TUNA: STATUS, TRENDS, AND ALTERNATIVE MANAGEMENT ARRANGEMENTS

Saul B. Saila
and
Virgil J. Norton

RFF Program of International Studies
of Fishery Arrangements

RFF/PISFA Paper 6

TUNA: STATUS, TRENDS, AND
ALTERNATIVE MANAGEMENT ARRANGEMENTS

WITHDRAWN

TUNA: STATUS, TRENDS, AND ALTERNATIVE MANAGEMENT ARRANGEMENTS

Saul B. Saila
and
Virgil J. Norton

Paper no. 6 in a series prepared for
THE PROGRAM OF INTERNATIONAL STUDIES OF
FISHERY ARRANGEMENTS
Francis T. Christy, Jr., Director

RESOURCES FOR THE FUTURE, INC.
Washington, D.C.

June 1974

Resources for the Future is a nonprofit corporation for research and education in the development, conservation, and use of natural resources and the improvement of the quality of the environment. It was established in 1952 with the cooperation of the Ford Foundation. Part of the work of Resources for the Future is carried out by its resident staff; part is supported by grants to universities and other nonprofit organizations. Unless otherwise stated, interpretations and conclusions in RFF publications are those of the authors; the organization takes responsibility for the selection of significant subjects for study, the competence of the researchers, and their freedom of inquiry. The manuscript was edited by Ruth B. Haas.

RFF editors: Mark Reinsberg, Joan R. Tron, Ruth B. Haas, Margaret Ingram

RFF—PISFA Paper 6. $3.00

Library of Congress Catalog Card Number 73-20846

ISBN 0-8018-1614-9

Figures

Tables

Preface

THE THIRD UNITED NATIONS CONFERENCE ON THE LAW OF THE SEA
is now scheduled to begin its first substantive sessions in 1974. Of
the many problems that the conference delegates will face, those
dealing with the management and distribution of marine fisheries
are among the most important, most difficult, and least understood. Almost all coastal states have an interest in marine
fisheries. Even though their interest may be peripheral, this
political constituency will have an influence on the decisions of
the delegations. The problems of fisheries are particularly difficult
because many stocks of fish have migratory patterns that extend
beyond the jurisdictions of single states. The migrations move
parallel with the coast into the waters of neighboring states or
outward into the high seas. With present trends toward the
dissolution of the principle of the "freedom of the seas" for
fishing, joint decisions on the distribution of the seas' wealth
become necessary. In the past, fishery decisions have usually
been made on specific problems by fishery experts. In the
forthcoming conference, however, decisions will be made in a
global arena, in the broad context of a multitude of ocean issues,
and by delegates with only a partial knowledge of fishery matters.

For these reasons Resources for the Future decided to
concentrate its current ocean interests on fisheries and, with the
help of a supplemental grant from the Ford Foundation, initiated
the Program of International Studies of Fishery Arrangements.
The objective of the program is to produce information that will
provide technical background for the UN Conference necessary
to the decision-making process. The program approach is to
concentrate primarily on particular fisheries and fishery regions,
attempting to elucidate the variety of alternatives that exist in
different, real situations. It is hoped that this approach will
contribute to a better understanding of the implications of the
proposals for universal regimes and principles that are likely to
emerge in the UN discussions. In addition, the program examines
some of the generic problems of fisheries management, distribution, and institutions.

Each study provides background information on recent developments and trends and a discussion of alternative legal and
institutional arrangements for the resolution of the problems. The

studies attempt to raise questions and suggest approaches that will be helpful to the decision makers, rather than to recommend specific courses of action. Every effort has been made to ensure that each study has been prepared from a non-national perspective and that it has taken into account all responsible points of view and interests. The studies are freely available to all delegates at the UN conference. In addition, the program seeks opportunities for full and free discussion of the studies with interested persons. Eventually, all of the separate studies may be put together in a single volume in order to meet the anticipated continuing demand for information on fishery arrangements. Comments and criticisms of the individual papers are solicited and will be considered for publication in such a volume.

Studies in the program include:

An overview of fishery arrangements;
North Pacific fisheries management;
East Central Atlantic fisheries;
Indian Ocean fisheries;
Southeast Asia fisheries;
World tuna fisheries;
Alternative international institutions;
Future fishery problems.

Each of the studies in the program illustrates a different kind of situation. The present study deals with problems of global significance that cannot be satisfactorily resolved on a regional basis. A rapidly increasing demand for tuna has led to a rapid growth in the number and size of tuna vessels, many of which are capable of fishing anywhere in the world's oceans. As conservation measures are applied in one area, they displace some of the fishing effort to other areas, thereby transferring pressures to other stocks already being threatened by overfishing. The necessity for coordinating management measures throughout the world is emphasized by the fact that present utilization is so great that, with one exception, each of the six major species of tuna in all of the three oceans is close to, or beyond, the point of maximum sustainable yield. And at the present rate of growth, it will be less than a decade to the time when the total capacity of the world's fleet of tuna vessels will be sufficient to take the total maximum average sustainable yields of all stocks.

In addition to the global ramifications, there are difficult problems for states within the different regions. Most species have wide-ranging migratory patterns which vary both seasonally and annually. They move freely both within and outside national jurisdictions and between national jurisdictions. There may be strong incentives for individual states to maximize their immediate gains from these migratory stocks, and to do so without regard to the long-term consequences. Such a race would be mutually destructive to the interests of both coastal and distant-water states. The prevention of these damages will require a high degree of foresight and cooperation among all interested parties.

These problems are addressed in this study by Saul B. Saila and Virgil J. Norton. Dr. Saila is professor of oceanography and zoology and director of the marine experiment station at the University of Rhode Island. Dr. Norton is professor of resource economics at the University of Rhode Island. Both Saila and Norton have conducted research and published extensively in their respective areas of fishery biology and fishery economics. In addition, they have served as consultants on fishery problems in many parts of the world.

FRANCIS T. CHRISTY, JR., Director
RFF Program of International
Studies of Fishery Arrangements

Acknowledgments

The authors wish to express appreciation to their sponsors, Resources for the Future, Inc., and The University of Rhode Island International Center for Marine Resources Development. We also wish to thank the many individuals who have assisted in making this report possible.

Included in this group are the following: F. T. Christy, Jr., RFF; J. A. Gulland and S. J. Holt, FAO; J. J. Joseph, Director, IATTC; B. J. Rothschild, Director, NMFS Southwest Fisheries Center; W. H. Lenarz, W. W. Fox, and R. M. Laurs, NMFS Southwest Fisheries Center; A. Felando, General Manager, American Tunaboat Association; J. M. Mason, Jr., and F. J. Mather, WHOI; and M. Kravjana, NMFS, Washington, D.C.

The generosity of these individuals with their time and ideas has helped us immeasurably. However, we alone must be held in account for errors we may have made in the preparation of this report.

Saul B. Saila
Virgil J. Norton

I Introduction

OWING TO THE INTERRELATIONSHIPS of the various tuna species—both at
the fishing level and in the world markets—an appropriate discussion
of the world tuna situation is not easily categorized. An attempt is
made in this report to organize the extensive information available in
such a way that summaries of catch, effort, yield potential, and
consumption are presented along with an evaluation of some alternative management arrangements.

It is important to note that much of the information in this report is
based on studies by individuals who have been involved intensively in
tuna research. Among these are J. J. Joseph, J. A. Gulland, B. J.
Rothschild, R. S. Shomura, G. C. Broadhead, F. W. Bell, and many
others. The intent of this report is to summarize the various available
studies and to draw from them certain broad implications for management programs.

MAJOR TUNA MARKET SPECIES

According to Joseph (1973), current tuna fisheries are based
primarily on six species—yellowfin (*Thunnus albacares*), albacore
(*T. alalunga*), bluefins (*T. thynnus* and *T. maccoyii*), bigeye (*T.
obesus*), and skipjack (*Katsuwonus pelamis*). These six major
market species presently comprise about 75 percent of the world
catch (figure 1) and nearly 100 percent of the international trade
of tuna and tunalike species. This report deals primarily with
these six species.

There are about thirty-five secondary market species of tunalike
fishes. Most important among these are bonito (*Sarda* spp.),
which are harvested in various regional fisheries. Also important
are other smaller tuna and related species including frigate
mackerel (*Auxis thazard*), little tunas (*Euthynnus* spp.), and
blackfin (*T. atlanticus* and *T. tongoll*). Although these secondary
market species are of substantial local importance, they are given
only limited consideration in this report.

The six major market species of tuna can be divided into two
geographic groups—tropical and temperate.[1] Tropical tuna species

---

[1] A detailed review of the biology of the various species mentioned above has
been provided by the World Scientific Meeting on the Biology of Tuna and
Related Species (FAO, 1963). For that reason, only certain elements of the
biology of the tunas are included in this paper.

Figure 1. Total catch of tunas and tunalike species, as compiled by the FAO, grouped within categories of economic importance, for 1952–71.

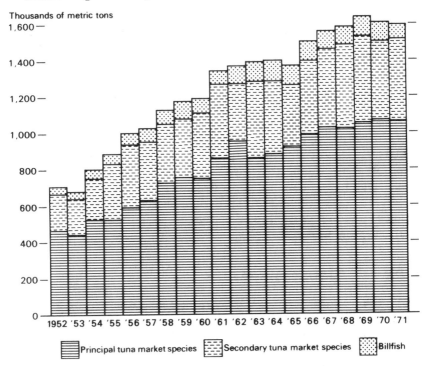

include yellowfin, skipjack, and bigeye; temperate species are the albacore and bluefins. The temperate tunas tend to grow more slowly and live longer than the tropical species. Although the bigeye and yellowfin tunas grow to a large size (up to 100 kilograms or more), they are relatively short lived, with a total life span of 5 years or less (Joseph, 1973). The skipjack is smaller than the other two tropical species and rarely reaches 15 kilograms in weight. It too is short lived compared with the temperate tunas.

The fact that tunas are wide ranging in their migrations adds to the complexity of appropriate management schemes. The trans-oceanic migrations of some tuna species (Atlantic bluefin and albacore in particular) have been documented. The International Commission for the Conservation of Atlantic Tunas (ICCAT) reports movements of Atlantic bluefin between the eastern coast of the United States and Canada to the Bay of Biscay and

Norwegian waters. The southern bluefin apparently migrates from spawning areas around Australia to the Atlantic, Pacific, and Indian oceans. The albacore and skipjack are also reported to migrate extensively. Presently available information suggests that the yellowfin and bigeye tuna make somewhat less extensive migrations than the other major tuna species (Joseph, 1973).

Blackburn (1965) has suggested that the bluefin, albacore, yellowfin, and bigeye tuna have a vertical depth range from the surface to at least 150 meters. Skipjack, however, are not regarded as commonly occurring below 70 meters. These tunas seem to have the same general depth range in the high seas as well as over the continental shelves.

The degree of separation, if any, between stocks of the various tuna species has not yet been adequately resolved. There is limited evidence (FAO, 1968) that albacore may be divided into a northern and a southern contingent in the Atlantic Ocean, and that the southern group migrates between the Atlantic and Indian oceans. Information on stock identification of the bigeye tuna seems entirely lacking at present. Existing information for bluefin implies there may be some overlap between southern and northern stocks in the Atlantic Ocean.

Figures 2–6 illustrate the general distribution of the major market species of tuna.[2]

MAJOR TUNA FISHERIES

The tuna fisheries of the world can be divided into two major groups: the longline fisheries, primarily of Japan, Republic of Korea, and Taiwan, and the surface fisheries, in which the United States and Japan are major participants. The surface fisheries use live bait and purse seines.

The longline fishery takes the largest quantity of tuna and tuna-like fishes. This technique, which involves setting main lines, each containing branch lines with a total of up to 2,000 hooks, is used for taking tuna at great depths. Longlining is generally considered to be relatively selective in fish size because this fishery tends to concentrate on larger fish.

Live bait fishing, which takes place on the surface, is second in importance. It generally is carried out closer to shore than

[2] The estimated distribution of the major market species presented in figures 2 through 6 is based primarily on Yabe, Yabuta, and Ueyanagi (1963); Laevastu and Rosa (1963); and Brock (1959).

Figure 2. Estimated distribution of albacore tuna.

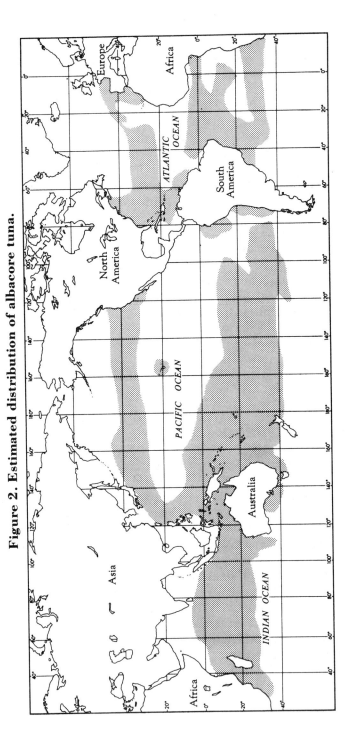

Figure 3. Estimated distribution of bigeye tuna.

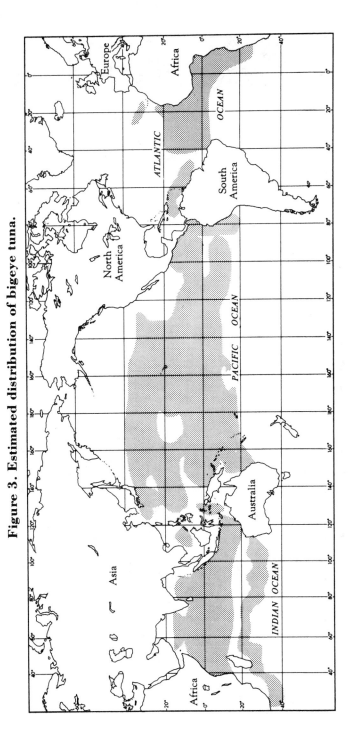

Figure 4. Estimated distribution of yellowfin tuna.

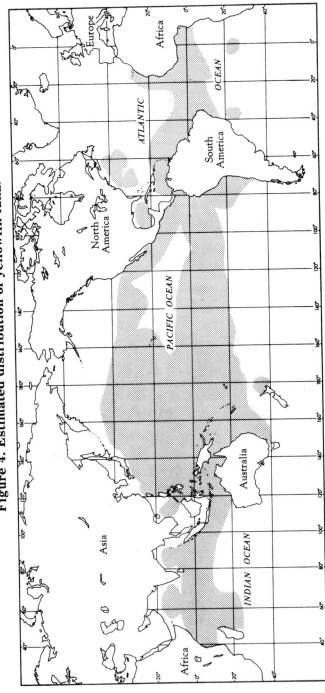

Figure 5. Estimated distribution of skipjack tuna.

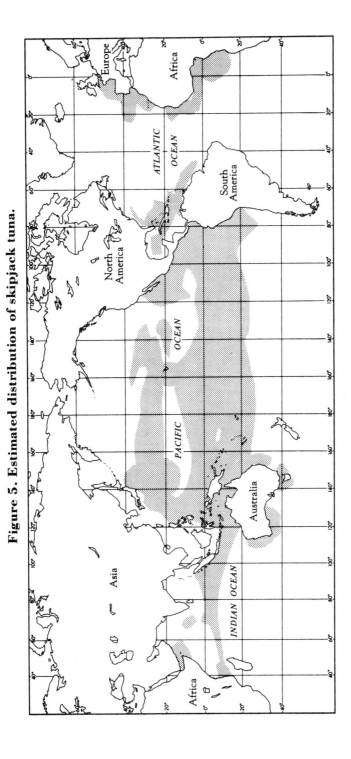

Figure 6. Estimated distribution of bluefin tuna.

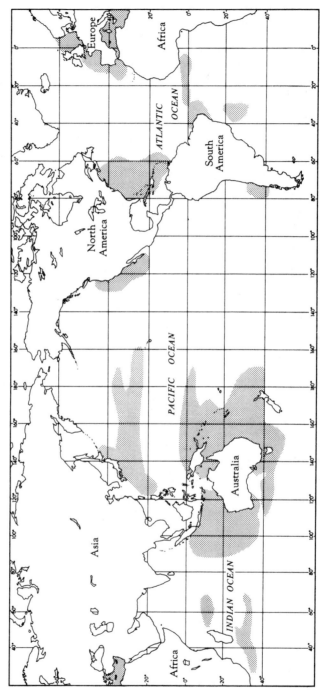

8

longline fishery because of the problem of maintaining the live
bait used to attract and concentrate the tunas. Poles with lines
and hooks on short lines are manned by one or two individuals.
When schools of tuna are found, the crewmen work fast and hard,
often for many hours, to hook and land as many tuna as possible
before the schools dissipate. This type of fishery is considered to
be extremely difficult and arduous work.

The purse seine, a highly efficient method of surface fishery, is
rapidly replacing bait fishery in certain areas. This technique
involves the use of a large net, which is used to surround the tuna
schools. The net is then drawn shut at the bottom to prevent the
tunas from escaping, pulled to the boat, and the tunas taken on
board. This technique is quite capital intensive compared with the
relatively labor-intensive longline and especially the live bait
method. The purse seine fishery does have certain constraints in
that the most effective fishing takes place where the thermocline is
relatively shallow. This is necessary to prevent large quantities of
tuna from escaping as the net is set and the bottom drawn shut.
Of the three techniques mentioned here, the purse seine is the
least selective with respect to fish size.

Although there are about forty nations involved in tuna fishing,
Japan, the United States, Taiwan, the Republic of Korea,
France, and Spain account for over 80 percent of the catch of the
six major market species. Joseph (1972, 1973) has summarized the
catch by nation as given in table 1.

The catch statistics reported in table 1 show a decline in the

Table 1. Catch of the Six Major Market Tuna Species, by Country, 1970 and 1971

Country	1970		1971	
	000 metric tons	%	000 metric tons	%
Japan	481.6	44.6	468.0	38.6
United States	225.3	20.8	238.6	19.7
Taiwan	103.7	9.6	101.9	8.4
Republic of Korea	73.0	6.8	73.8	6.1
France	50.3	4.7	71.6	5.9
Spain	50.0	4.6	49.8	4.1
Subtotal	983.9	91.1	1,003.7	82.8
Others	122.1	8.9	208.8	17.2
Total	1,106.0	100.0	1,212.5	100.0

Source: Joseph (1972, 1973).

9

Japanese catch of major tuna species, reflecting a trend which has been occurring since 1962 (Asada, 1972). During this period, however, most other nations have recorded increases in tuna landings, bringing about a rather rapid increase in total world catch.

Table 2 shows the approximate catch by nation in each of the three oceans. Japan is the leading tuna fishing nation in the Pacific and Indian oceans, while France is currently the leading nation in the Atlantic Ocean.

The composition of the catch by species as reported by Joseph (1972, 1973) is given in table 3. An examination of this table shows that in 1971 skipjack replaced yellowfin as the most

Table 2. Approximate Total Catch of Tuna in 1970, by Country and by Ocean

Country	Catch (000 metric tons)				
	Pacific Ocean	Atlantic Ocean	Indian Ocean	Total[a]	% of total[a]
Japan	393.5	38.8	49.3	481.6	43
United States[b]	203.3	18.8	0.0	222.1	20
Taiwan	51.0	24.6	27.8	103.4	10
Republic of Korea	32.8	18.2	22.0	73.0	7
France	0.0	49.4	0.0	49.4	5
Spain	0.0	41.1	0.0	41.1	4
Others	57.0	57.8	1.8	116.6	11
Total	737.6	248.7	100.9	1,087.2	100

Source: FAO (1971b).

a These data do not conform exactly to those reported by Joseph (1972). (See table 1.)

b Figures include Puerto Rican landings.

Table 3. Composition of Catch, by Species for Selected Years *(percent)*

Species	1962	1963	1969	1970	1971
Yellowfin	28.0	26.3	32.6	31.6	25.3
Skipjack	26.6	21.5	25.3	29.2	36.1
Albacore	19.8	23.3	20.0	18.4	19.1
Bigeye	14.4	15.6	12.5	11.1	12.0
Bluefin (northern and southern)	11.2	13.3	9.6	9.7	7.5
Total	100.0	100.0	100.0	100.0	100.0
Total thousand metric tons	905.0	859.0	1,100.0	1,100.0	1,212.5

Source: Joseph (1972, 1973).

important species. Since 1963 there has been a gradual decline in the proportion of the catch made up by bluefin and bigeye tunas.

Japan and the United States account for approximately 60 percent of the total world catch of the major market species of tuna (see table 2). An understanding of the world tuna situation therefore requires an examination of the development and current status of the fleets of these two nations. This is also useful because, to a large extent, the rapidly growing fleets of Taiwan and the Republic of Korea have been patterned after the Japanese fleet. The expanding fleets of France and Spain have followed a developmental pattern similar to that of the United States.

Japan

Although the tuna catch of the Japanese fleet has been declining during the past decade, Japan still accounts for almost 40 percent of the world catch of major market tuna species. The Japanese tuna fleet is the largest and most cosmopolitan in the world, harvesting significant quantities in the Atlantic, Indian, and Pacific oceans.

The Japanese tuna fleet consists of approximately 3,000 vessels with a total gross tonnage of almost 400,000 tons. Of these, approximately half operate in Japanese waters. The Japanese deep-sea tuna fleet consists of about 1,200 vessels which are primarily longliners with a gross tonnage of almost 300,000 tons. In addition, the Japanese have approximately 40 mother-ship operations which fish in all three oceans (Japan Tuna Fisheries Federation, 1969). Each mother ship forms the nucleus for a fleet operation involving several smaller catching vessels. Catches from these vessels are taken on board the mother ship for processing and/or freezing. This type of operation is extremely mobile and since the catcher vessels do not have to return to shore for unloading their catch, the mother-ship fleets can remain at sea for several months at a time. Many thousand fishermen are employed on these Japanese vessels, with crew sizes ranging from 35 to 40 men for large longliners and 70 for the mother ships.

According to Asada (1973, p. 16), the Japanese government issues licenses for deep-sea tuna fishing. Through these licenses the government controls tuna fishing by the industry. Asada reports that the licenses are transferable and

are usually purchased through brokers engaged in this business. Purchases are made on the basis of price per vessel ton. The more profitable the fishery or the more advantageous the enlargement of the vessel, the higher the prices, and these therefore fluctuate according to the state of the fishery. For example, the price per ton for deep-sea tuna vessels rose each year until 1963 when it reached U.S. $1500, but fell to U.S. $470 in 1965, reflecting the deteriorating profitability of the fishery as a result of the decrease in the resource and the fall in tuna prices. Recently, it has risen again to more than U.S. $1000. Licenses are regarded as the property of their holders. Thus, although it is possible for fishermen/entrepreneurs to increase the number of their vessels, to enlarge the size of vessels, or to enter a licensed fishery, costs are considerable, and constitute a financial burden on the enterprise.

Considering that the deep-sea tuna fleet totals approximately 300,000 gross tons, the current property value of these licenses totals approximately 300 million dollars (U.S.). This represents an average license value of about $250,000 (U.S.) per vessel in the Japanese deep-sea tuna fleet. This situation provides an excellent example of how limiting access to a common property resource can result in "property rights" which can be valued and exchanged in the market. The establishment of such a property right is an essential prerequisite to preventing significant economic waste in ocean fisheries.

In recent years the catch rates for the Japanese longliners fishing for certain species such as southern bluefin have declined significantly. This has contributed to the generally increasing costs per pound of fish landed by the fleet. The rapid growth of the Japanese economy has also resulted in significantly higher labor and gear costs. These factors, combined with the far-ranging nature of the Japanese operation, have induced the Japanese industry to establish bases in foreign countries and to enter into agreements which allow the Japanese access to lower cost foreign labor and capital, particularly with Taiwan, the Republic of Korea, and Malaysia (Moal, 1972 and Asada, 1972). The Japanese fleets land and/or transship tuna at numerous points in the Pacific, Atlantic, and Indian oceans (Japanese Tuna Fisheries Federation, 1969).

In spite of these landing and transshipment arrangements and rapid increases in the price of tuna, the Japanese fleet seems to find it extremely difficult to maintain the profit margins of earlier years. In particular, competition with the expanding fleets of nations such as Taiwan and the Republic of Korea, which among other things generally have lower labor costs, is a growing problem for Japan.

United States

The U.S. tuna fleet accounts for about 20 percent of the world landings of the major market species. Most of this catch comes

12

from the eastern Pacific and is made up primarily of yellowfin, skipjack, and albacore.

United States tuna fishing, in contrast to Japanese longline fishery, consists almost totally of surface fishery. During the 1950s the U.S. fleet was made up of live bait vessels, but since 1961 the major catching capacity of the fleet has changed to a highly mobile purse-seining fleet that no longer must rely on coastal bait sources. Vessels in this fleet are now capable of fishing for tuna in any area of the world.

In the United States there are over 7,000 tuna fishermen operating on more than 2,000 vessels. This figure includes many small vessels that fish along the West Coast of the United States. Approximately 75 percent of the U.S. catch, however, is taken by less than 150 purse seiners operating in the eastern tropical Pacific and to some extent in the Atlantic—primarily off the western coast of Africa.

The development of the purse seiner, along with restrictions on catch of yellowfin in much of the eastern Pacific, has resulted in many U.S. vessels entering the Atlantic tuna fishery. (This will be explained in more detail in a later section.) The tuna fleet is currently the most modern and far-ranging fishing fleet based in the United States. These modern vessels, however, represent a very large capital investment and if increasing worldwide effort on tunas results in declining catch rates, these vessels owners will

Table 4. U.S. Flag Bait Boats and Seiners Operating in IATTC Area[a]

Year	Bait boats		Seiners		Total	
	No. of vessels	Bait boat capacity	No. of vessels	Seiner capacity	Vessels	Capacity
1962	40	5,885	115	30,636	155	36,521
1963	59	3,825	119	36,504	178	40,329
1964	36	3,267	118	37,249	154	40,516
1965	44	3,980	118	38,059	162	42,039
1966	51	4,794	108	35,945	159	40,739
1967	47	4,419	106	36,932	153	41,351
1968	50	4,644	109	41,338	159	45,982
1969	43	4,077	120	49,093	163	53,170
1970	44	3,827	121	56,179	165	60,006
1971	48	3,770	124	69,790	172	73,560

Source: IATTC unpublished report, 9–14–72.
[a] See table 13 for information on total international fleet operating in IATTC area 1962–73.

likely find it more and more difficult to maintain an adequate return on their investment.

Table 4 summarizes the U.S. vessels fishing in the Eastern Pacific Inter-American Tropical Tuna Commission (IATTC) area.

II Major Ocean Fisheries

THE FOLLOWING DISCUSSIONS of the tuna fisheries by major ocean areas are included to provide some historical background and a brief description of the present condition of tuna stocks. In each case the order of discussion of the six major species is the same to allow easier comparison among the sections. Thus, the order does not necessarily indicate relative importance in each ocean area.

According to Joseph (1973), the distribution of the world catch of tuna in 1971 was as follows: Atlantic Ocean, 24.3 percent; Indian Ocean, 13.4 percent; and Pacific Ocean, 62.3 percent.

ATLANTIC OCEAN

Certain of the Atlantic Ocean tuna fisheries which utilize traps, harpoons, and trolling extend back in time over hundreds of years. However, the beginning of significant increases in the exploitation of tuna and tunalike fishes in the Atlantic Ocean dates from the mid-1950s, when the Japanese began longline and the French began surface fisheries. According to Shomura (1966), the Japanese commercial fleet began fishing in the tropical Atlantic in 1957. In 1956 the total catch of tuna from the Atlantic Ocean was about 81,000 metric tons. By 1963, only 7 years later, the catch had tripled to more than 257,000 metric tons. The catch has remained at about that level since then (table 5).

During the early years of the fishery, the Japanese longline vessels were unchallenged by other nations, but in the past decade vessels from the Republic of Korea and Taiwan have entered longline fishery in increasing numbers. The Japanese Atlantic Ocean tuna catch reached a maximum in 1965, but has declined since that time to a current level of around 40,000 metric tons. Increased catches by other countries have approximately offset the declining catch by Japan (table 5).

At present the tuna fisheries of the Atlantic are carried out by both longlines and surface gear. Longline vessels, because of their flexibility in fishing at various depths, move from one part of the Atlantic Ocean to another during a single season and represent a truly high-seas fishery. On the other hand, as was indicated in

Table 5. Atlantic Ocean Catch of Major Tuna Species, by Country for 1965 and 1970

(000 metric tons)

Country	Bluefin 1965	Bluefin 1970	Bigeye 1965	Bigeye 1970	Yellowfin 1965	Yellowfin 1970	Skipjack 1965	Skipjack 1970	Albacore 1965	Albacore 1970	Total 1965	Total 1970
Japan	9.5	4.4	28.6	8.8	37.9	6.7	6.3	7.5	42.6	11.4	124.9	38.8
United States[a]	3.2	2.8	0.0	0.0	0.0	14.0	0.0	2.0	0.0	0.0	3.2	18.8
Taiwan	0.0	0.2	0.0	5.3	0.1	7.2	0.0	0.0	0.1	11.9	0.2	24.6
France	1.2	0.9	0.0	0.0	24.0	31.3	0.0	10.6	16.6	6.6	41.8	49.4
Republic of Korea	0.0	0.0	0.2	0.2	0.0	5.0	0.0	0.0	1.0	13.0	1.2	18.2
Spain[b]	9.2	17.5	0.0	0.0	0.0	0.0	0.2	0.0	29.0	23.6	38.4	41.1
Others[b]	8.7	7.7	2.6	2.1	16.9	22.2	7.5	16.5	8.8	9.3	44.5	57.8
Total	31.8	33.5	31.4	16.4	78.9	86.4	14.0	36.6	98.1	75.8	254.2	248.7

Source: FAO (1971b).

[a] U.S. figures include landings at Puerto Rico.

[b] Species composition reported for Spain and for "others" may not be reliable. Also, the data reported for 1970 for Spain are 8.9 thousand metric tons less than reported by Joseph (1972).

16

chapter I, surface fishery is usually confined to areas over or close to the continental shelf. Since about 1967 a United States fleet of large purse seiners has participated in the West African tuna fishery. The United States fleet of purse seiners operating off the African Coast expanded from three vessels in 1967 to twenty-four in 1971 (Sakagawa and Lenarz, 1972). This expansion is related directly to the yellowfin regulations in the eastern tropical Pacific.

The species composition of the entire Atlantic tuna fishery has undergone marked changes in recent years. Table 5 shows that there have been significant drops in the landings of bigeye and albacore but increases in catch of the other major species, especially skipjack.

Major Atlantic Ocean Species

Yellowfin. Yellowfin tuna were not commercially exploited in the Atlantic prior to 1956. Yellowfin catch statistics and results from models of yield-per-recruit and relative stock fecundity in the Atlantic now indicate that further increases in fishing activities will result in only small increases in the catch, a significant decline in catch-per-unit effort, and a possible decrease in reproduction (Hayasi, 1972). The yield of yellowfin tuna in the Atlantic Ocean did not substantially increase from 1968 to 1971 in spite of rapid growth in fishing intensity. An indication of the concern about this species is represented by the fact that at the Fourth Plenary Session of the regular meeting of ICCAT a resolution was passed in which the commission authorized the council to recommend to the contracting parties that a minimum size regulation be established (ICCAT, 1971, p. 5).

Albacore. The albacore of the Atlantic Ocean are widely distributed between 45° N and 45° S. The primary albacore areas are the northern waters of the Atlantic (30°N), off the Cape of Good Hope, and off Montevideo, Uruguay. France and Spain currently pursue an active live bait and trolling fishery for albacore in the northeast Atlantic and take more than one third of the Atlantic catch of albacore. There has been an increase in fishing activity for albacore accompanied by a reduction in the hooking rate for longliners. It is believed that albacore are currently fully exploited (Joseph, 1973).

Bigeye. Studies on the natural history and stock assessment for bigeye are less advanced than they are for other tuna species in the Atlantic. The latitudinal distribution of bigeye extends in the Atlantic from about 50° south to 50° north. It is believed that the bigeye tuna in the Atlantic Ocean are nearly fully exploited.

Skipjack. Prior to 1963, only small amounts of skipjack were taken from the Atlantic. This fishery has recently developed rapidly due to the expansion of surface fishing activities and the increase in demand for skipjack in the European market. The skipjack resource of the Atlantic Ocean is believed to be large and not yet fully exploited (FAO, 1968). Much of the purse seine catch of skipjack is taken in the Gulf of Guinea and relatively close inshore. In addition, areas off Angola (south of 10°S) have recently yielded substantial catches of skipjack. The beginning date of the summer and fall skipjack fishery by United States purse seiners is influenced by the date that yellowfin catch quotas in the tropical Pacific Ocean are met. This is one important indication of the global nature of the major tuna fleets and a reason why, as will be discussed later, a global approach is needed for effective tuna management.

Bluefin. The bluefin migrates along both coasts of the Atlantic. Bluefin are the only tuna common in Norwegian waters and are believed to be the most temperature tolerant of the major tuna species.
There is considerable concern that the established Norwegian, Guinean, Spanish, and Portuguese bluefin fisheries are on the verge of collapse. These fisheries have traditionally consisted of large fish, and it is contended that recruitment into the large (200 kilogram and greater) size classes has been reduced by current purse seining and longlining techniques. Scientists of member nations of ICCAT are concerned that the bluefin may be overexploited.

Summary. It appears that in the Atlantic Ocean only the skipjack represent a significant potential for increased landings among the six major species. Effort levels for the other species are currently high enough that any additional effort is likely to be damaging both biologically and economically. There does, however, seem to be a reasonable potential for a blackfin fishery in the Caribbean Sea, and an increasingly active fishery by Cuba for skipjack and blackfin tuna is developing. France has also started a new purse seine fishery for skipjack in the Caribbean and is experiencing moderate success.

INDIAN OCEAN

Although traditional near-shore fisheries for tuna have been known in the Indian Ocean for years, the development of the open ocean fishery is comparatively recent. The first successful fishery for yellowfin tuna in the Indian Ocean was begun in 1952 by the Japanese. Since then, there has been a significant expansion in the number of vessels and areas of operation. In addition to Japan, the Republic of Korea and Taiwan have established important fisheries for the major tuna fishes in the Indian Ocean. The range of major tuna fishing activities extends from approximately 15° north latitude to 35° south latitude, from which about 100,000 metric tons of the major tuna species were taken in 1970.

In 1965, Japan accounted for over 90 percent of the Indian Ocean catch of the major tunas. By 1970, the combination of a declining Japanese catch and the rapidly expanding fleets of other nations resulted in a significant reordering of the relative catch (table 6).

In addition to the major tunas, much interest and activity has developed in various tunalike species. Landings from the growing surface fishery for tuna and tunalike fishes were 84.3 thousand metric tons in 1970. Sri Lanka has led in the capture of various tunalike fishes from surface fisheries, with a total of 33.9 thousand metric tons in 1970. In India the traditional fisheries for tuna around the Minicoy and Laccadive Island group have existed at low levels for years. During 1970 India reported 3.1 thousand metric tons of tunalike fishes consisting primarily of skipjack and *Euthynnus*. A large-scale Indian boat-building program is envisaged around the Laccadive Islands, which is expected to increase Indian tuna catches significantly (Dwivedi, 1972).

Major Indian Ocean Species

Yellowfin. The yellowfin was the first Indian Ocean tuna species exploited heavily. Yellowfin seem to occur in greatest densities between 10° north and 10° south latitude, with higher concentrations in the western area. It is believed to be near its upper limit for rational exploitation at this time. The report of the IOFC/IFPC *Ad Hoc* Working Party of Scientists on Stock Assessment of Tuna (FAO/1OFC/IPFC, 1972) concluded that increased effort would not increase the landings of yellowfin.

Table 6. Indian Ocean Catch of Major Tuna Species, by Country for 1965 and 1970

(000 metric tons)

Country	Bluefin 1965	Bluefin 1970	Bigeye 1965	Bigeye 1970	Yellowfin 1965	Yellowfin 1970	Skipjack 1965	Skipjack 1970	Albacore 1965	Albacore 1970	Total 1965	Total 1970
Japan	21.7	19.5	15.5	12.5	20.9	10.9	0.1	0.1	14.2	6.3	72.4	49.3
Taiwan	0.0	0.1	1.3	5.3	2.2	14.8	0.0	0.0	0.0	7.6	3.5	27.8
Republic of Korea	0.0	0.0	0.1	1.7	0.0	3.3	0.0	0.0	0.5	2.3	0.6	7.3
Others[a]	0.0	0.0	0.7	1.3	7.6	10.8	30.6	43.4	0.7	1.4	39.6	56.9
Total	21.7	19.6	17.6	20.8	30.7	39.8	30.7	43.5	15.4	17.6	116.1	141.3

Source: FAO (1971b), as adjusted by data from FAO/IOFC/IPFC (1972) and personal communication with J. A. Gulland.

[a] Much of the catch recorded under this category is made by India and Maldives.

Albacore. Most albacore are caught south of 10° south latitude. Albacore seem to be found at maximum densities in the southwestern sector, where they extend at times beyond 40° south latitude. The albacore has been under intensive exploitation for some time, and an increase in longline effort will probably not result in substantially increased catches.

Bigeye. This species is distributed in two major zones in the Indian Ocean—one in tropical equatorial waters between the equator and 10° south and the other south of 30° south latitude. The potential for this species is believed to be nearly realized. The IOFC/IFPC working party concluded in 1972 that an estimated maximum sustainable yield (MSY) of 30,000–32,000 metric tons is possible. This is only about 2,000 metric tons greater than the estimated 1970 catch. It is not believed that a significant surface fishery can develop for this species.

Skipjack. Of the major tuna species, only the skipjack is believed to be underutilized in the Indian Ocean. Gulland (1970) has estimated a potential catch of 160,000–300,000 metric tons. This is contrasted with a 1970 yield of 43,500 metric tons, reported in table 6. It is anticipated that skipjack will predominate in the Indian Ocean catch in the future in a manner similar to that which seems to be occurring in the Atlantic.

Bluefin. The southern bluefin tuna is found primarily in the southern portions of the Indian Ocean. The fishery for this species extends from portions of Australia to South Africa. As with most other major tuna species in the Indian Ocean, there is reason to believe that the southern bluefin is currently overexploited.

Summary. The longline fisheries for the major tuna species in the Indian Ocean appear to have reached or nearly reached levels of maximum production. The interactions between longline and surface fisheries are not well understood. Thus, the effect of an increasing surface fishery on these species is not known. With the exception of skipjack, however, little can probably be expected from these species in terms of increased catch. An increase in the yield of skipjack by a factor of about three seems possible. The tunalike fishes, such as bonito and frigate mackerels, represent a fairly large but unmeasured potential for developing fisheries near coastlines.

PACIFIC OCEAN

The fishery for tuna in the Pacific Ocean has existed since ancient times. This is especially true for skipjack, which has formed an important part of the Japanese diet for many years. At the end of World War I, Japan acquired Germany's holdings in the Pacific, and throughout the 1920s spent considerable time and money evaluating the fishery resources potential for the Pacific island area. During the 1930s fishing bases involving both longline and live-bait tuna catching operations were established on several islands. Substantial catches (up to 35,000 metric tons) of skipjack were taken by the Japanese in the Trust Territory of the Pacific Islands prior to World War II.

From the end of World War II to about 1952, the Japanese fishery, consisting of local bait fishery and longlining vessels, was confined to the western and central Pacific Ocean. During this period the major longlining tuna fishing effort was concentrated south of the equator. From 1957 to 1964 Japanese longlining effort increased in the eastern Pacific Ocean, but it has declined during the past decade.

Although tuna fishing was introduced into Taiwan in 1931 by the Japanese, this fishery was conducted in coastal waters until 1959, after which the Taiwan fleet (primarily longlining) registered significant catches in the Pacific Ocean.

In the eastern Pacific, the United States tuna industry had its beginnings in California in 1903. The albacore fishery off the western coast of the United States is seasonal, with most of the fish being found near shore in the summer and fall. The growth of the United States tuna fishery was relatively slow until the 1950s, when a considerable expansion in bait-boat operations took place. The most recent expansion by the United States fleet has involved large purse seiners. At present, the United States has about 70 percent of the eastern Pacific fleet capacity and catches about 80 percent of all tuna caught in that area.

At this time the Pacific Ocean catch of the principal market species of tunas is the highest of any ocean area, amounting to approximately 755,000 metric tons in 1971 (Joseph, 1973), or almost 60 percent of the world catch of the major market species. Japan and the United States account for over three-fourths of the total catch of the major tuna species in the Pacific Ocean (table 7).

Major Pacific Ocean Species

Yellowfin. The efforts of the Inter-American Tropical Tuna Commission (IATTC) have been directed primarily to yellowfin

22

Table 7. Pacific Ocean Catch of Major Tuna Species, by Country for 1965 and 1970

(000 metric tons)

Country	Bluefin		Bigeye		Yellowfin		Skipjack		Albacore		Total	
	1965	1970	1965	1970	1965	1970	1965	1970	1965	1970	1965	1970
Japan	24.5	20.0	66.2	71.0	65.0	61.4	129.6	195.3	70.5	45.8	355.8	393.5
United States[a]	7.6	4.8	0.0	0.0	76.6	126.2	64.7	46.8	16.9	25.5	165.8	203.3
Taiwan	0.0	0.0	2.0	5.0	4.9	14.3	13.0	14.9	1.7	16.8	21.6	51.0
Republic of Korea	0.0	0.0	0.7	1.8	2.0	10.0	0.0	0.0	3.5	21.0	6.2	32.8
Others	10.3	10.2	0.0	0.0	3.9	16.4	29.9	29.0	0.3	1.4	48.7	57.0
Total	42.4	35.0	68.9	77.8	152.4	228.3	237.2	286.0	92.9	110.5	597.0	737.6

Source: FAO (1971b).
[a] U.S. figures include landings at Puerto Rico.

conservation. Overall catch quotas for the IATTC-regulated area have been established. The shortcomings of this regulation and the widespread effects of IATTC region quotas upon fisheries in other oceans are becoming increasingly apparent. This problem is discussed in detail in a later section of this report. It should be emphasized, however, that the relative abundance of yellowfin in the IATTC region has remained high.

A controlled experimental program involving increasing quotas has been in effect for several years. The total quota system in this region, with no country quotas or limits on entry, and the resulting increasingly large size and efficiency of the fleet have reduced the length of the fishing season. It should be noted that the IATTC has recently initiated certain country quotas, primarily to allow for new entrants into the fishery and to protect certain of the fleets with smaller vessels that have no alternate fishing areas.

It has been estimated by the IATTC that in 1973 during the yellowfin season there were 272 vessels active in the regulated area. These included vessels from Bermuda, Canada, Costa Rica, Ecuador, France, Mexico, Panama, Peru, Spain, the United States, Japan, and the Netherlands (see table 13). A decade ago the U.S. fleet represented about 90 percent of the capacity operating in this area. Currently the U.S. fleet represents about 70 percent of the capacity.

Albacore. The albacore ranks third in landings among the major market species in the Pacific Ocean. Here it seems to consist of two separate populations—one in areas south of the equator and another in the North Pacific. In the 1950s the albacore fishery consisted of summer trolling and pole-and-line fishing of the coast of North America, winter longline fishing in the western North Pacific, and spring pole-and-line fishing in the western North Pacific. The fishery in the South Pacific has been developed primarily by the Japanese, where the intensity increased for some time, but has recently declined. Both of the above-mentioned areas demonstrate a decline in apparent abundance as indicated by catch rates. According to Joseph (1973), albacore tuna appear to be fully exploited at present.

Bigeye. This species has a wide distribution in the Pacific Ocean, with apparent centers of abundance east of the Philippines. Bigeye landings are fourth in importance in current catches from the Pacific. Bigeye are believed to be fully exploited in the Pacific Ocean at present.

Skipjack. Skipjack tuna is currently the major species caught in the Pacific Ocean. There is a rapid acceleration in efforts to further develop the skipjack tuna fisheries in the central and western Pacific (Hester and Otsu, 1973). The potential yield of skipjack has been variously estimated over a wide range. Joseph (1973) has suggested that the global potential for skipjack is considerably higher than the present catch, but that this species may be near the limit of sustainable yield in the western Pacific area. According to Blackburn and Laurs (1972), most of the skipjack fishery in the eastern Pacific lies within a few hundred miles of the coast, where the adolescent stages of a migratory population breeding in the central tropical Pacific are found. It seems evident that the United States tuna fishery in the eastern tropical Pacific is becoming more dependent upon skipjack tuna now than it has been in the past. The skipjack is believed to be separated into a western Pacific stock and a central Pacific stock that extends from the Carolinas and the eastern side of the Marianas to the Americas.

Bluefin. Anderson *et al.* (1953) described the Pacific distribution of bluefin tuna as ranging from Pt. Conception south to Peru and west to Hawaii, Japan, and Australia. There apparently are both east and west migrations of southern bluefin tuna from the vicinity of the Australian breeding grounds. These fish are truly global in their distribution, fish from this source having been found in the three major oceans. For example, tagged bluefin have been shown to cross the Pacific Ocean from Baja to Japan (Clemens and Flittner, 1969). The stocks of both southern and northern bluefin are believed to be very heavily exploited (Joseph, 1973). The relatively large size at maturity and slow growth of both southern and northern bluefin probably explains the relatively low catches of the bluefins among the important Pacific Ocean market species.

Summary. The major tuna species in the Pacific Ocean, with the exception of skipjack, are believed to be fully exploited or overexploited. In spite of this, fishing effort, especially on yellowfin, continues to expand. This means the yellowfin season in the IATTC area will become even shorter—with the result that effort on other species and in other oceans will likewise expand. Other than skipjack, only the secondary market species are believed to represent a relatively large potential resource in the Pacific Ocean.

III World Markets for Tuna

TUNA AND TUNALIKE SPECIES are locally important as a source of protein for the peoples of many states and areas throughout the world.[1] However, most tunas—especially the six major market species of primary concern in this report—are consumed in the developed nations. Over 90 percent of the recorded world consumption of tuna takes place in the United States, Japan, and certain Western European states (table 8). Japan and the United States, which catch the major share of the world tuna landings, account for about three-fourths of the consumption of tuna.

Several factors combine to make tuna a food source that will continue to be utilized almost entirely in the higher income countries. First, tunas are high on the marine trophic web and the average sustainable yield is not as high as for certain other species such as herring or anchovies or even certain ground fishes. Second, the major market tuna species are widely dispersed in the Atlantic, Indian, and Pacific oceans, Harvesting operators therefore require large investments in high seas vessels and gear. Third, tuna products have a relatively high income elasticity. This means that as individual incomes increase, the desire for tuna increases, and as a result, prices tend to rise. Finally, most of the major market species are near or at the levels of full exploitation. Increased fishing effort therefore will tend to bring about declining catch rates, increasing costs per pound of tuna landed, and higher market prices necessary to cover these increasing costs. Considering the above factors and the fact that the major market tuna species are traded in a worldwide international market, it is unlikely that developing states can afford to compete at the market level with the higher income states for significant quantities of tuna. Either the protein per unit of currency or the foreign exchange forgone (in the case of those states that harvest tuna) will be too great. Therefore current world consumption patterns are expected to continue into the future.

The United States, the largest consumer of tuna, accounts for almost half of the world consumption of the major market species

---

[1] Broadhead (1971) and Broderick (1973) have provided excellent descriptions of the world tuna markets and the discussion in this chapter is based primarily on their reports.

Table 8. World Consumption of Tuna, by Country

(round weight, 000 metric tons)

Country	1960	1965	1969
United States	339.1	398.1	461.6
Japan	258.2	290.2	330.1
Western Europe	112.7	179.8	193.4
France	(31.8)	(41.6)	(50.5)
Spain	(23.9)	(41.1)	(29.4)
Italy	(40.1)	(53.3)	(62.6)
West Germany	(13.3)	(27.6)	(30.7)
Others	(3.6)	(16.2)	(20.2)
Subtotal	710.0	868.1	985.1
Others	53.0	55.9	95.9
Total	763.0	924.0	1,081.0

Source: Broadhead (1971) and Broderick (1973).

(table 8). Essentially all of the U.S. consumption is in the form of canned albacore, yellowfin, and skipjack tunas, with preferences and highest prices for albacore, which is sold as white meat tuna. The U.S. market accounts for approximately 70 percent of the world consumption of albacore.

Since the U.S. fishing fleet provides less than half of the tuna consumed, U.S. processors rely heavily on imports, mostly from Japan, in the form of frozen raw tuna or tuna canned in brine. Table 9 shows that the U.S. fleets have traditionally supplied about 40 percent of the U.S. market supply. In 1972, however, because of rapidly growing per capita consumption (up 21 percent over 1971) even a record U.S. catch of tuna supplied only about one-third of the total. Tuna imports into the United States in 1972 were valued at 250 million dollars—almost 100 million dollars greater than in 1971. Much of the imported raw tuna is canned in plants owned by U.S. interests in Puerto Rico and American Samoa.

Japan is the second largest consumer of tuna. In contrast to the United States, only a small portion of the Japanese consumption of tuna is in canned form. The Japanese consume tuna primarily in the form of marinated thin-sliced raw, smoked, or dried tuna. Prices for these products are generally very high, once again emphasizing the fact that most of the world tuna catch seems to be destined for the high income states. Although the per capita consumption of tuna in Japan is probably the world's highest, consumption during the past decade seems to have leveled off, both on a total and per capita basis. Currently, Japan exports, in either raw or canned form, almost one-third of its total tuna

Table 9. Source of U.S. Supply of Canned Tuna, 1962–72

(percent)

Year	U.S. pack from domestic landings[a]	U.S. pack from imported fresh and frozen tuna[b]	Imported canned
1962	37.6	47.9	14.5
1963	41.8	43.2	15.0
1964	38.1	48.4	13.5
1965	39.5	48.1	12.4
1966	33.6	52.9	13.5
1967	40.3	45.3	14.4
1968	38.1	47.4	14.5
1969	38.6	45.9	15.5
1970	39.9	45.9	14.2
1971	39.1	48.9	12.0
1972	34.2	57.4	8.4

Source: U.S. Department of Commerce (1973).

[a] Includes pack from landings in Puerto Rico and American Samoa by U.S. vessels.

[b] Includes tuna from foreign suppliers canned in American Samoa.

catch, with about 60 percent of these exports going to the United States. Japan also exports large quantities of canned tuna to West Germany and raw tuna to Italy.

The third major market area for tuna is Western Europe. Consumption in each nation is fairly low, but total annual consumption is now well over 200,000 metric tons and has been increasing at a fairly rapid rate. France and Spain, with important Atlantic Ocean fleets, are largely self-sufficient, while the other countries, especially West Germany and Italy, must rely on imports.

Although the United States, Japan, and certain Western European countries account for most of the world consumption of tuna, there are important and, in some cases, rapidly growing markets for tuna in countries such as Taiwan, the Republic of Korea, Portugal, Mexico, Australia, Canada, and Turkey.

Summary

The international trade flows of tuna amount to the equivalent of about 500 million U.S. dollars annually. Japan is the major exporting nation, but the Republic of Korea, Taiwan, Spain, Portugal, Norway, France, Peru, and Canada also export significant quantities of tuna.

Primary importing nations are the United States, Italy, West

Germany, Canada, the United Kingdom, Switzerland, and Yugoslavia.

Tuna is consumed in many nations, but most of the products from the six major market tuna species are sold in the United States, Japan, and Western Europe. Therefore, although these tunas may represent important protein sources in other localized areas, consumption is concentrated in the higher income nations. Because of the relatively high prices of tuna, this pattern will most likely hold in the future.

IV Potential Catch from the World Oceans and Future Demand for Tuna

POTENTIAL CATCH OF THE MAJOR TUNA SPECIES

JOSEPH (1973, p. 13) summarizes the general status of the world tuna stocks as follows:

> . . . most of the principal market species of tuna are nearly or fully exploited. Yellowfin, albacore, and bigeye tuna appear to be nearly fully exploited, and increased effort on these species will result in small, if any, increased catches and could even result in decreased catches. Northern bluefin tuna in the Pacific Ocean are probably fully exploited, and in the Atlantic Ocean are possibly overexploited. Albacore tuna appear to be fully exploited in all three oceans and increased production is not likely. Southern bluefin tuna has been heavily exploited in recent years and catches have declined by about 30 percent. . . . [Skipjack] appears to be abundant relative to the other principal tunas, and to be underexploited throughout most of its range; thus, present production might be substantially increased. A possible exception to this is in the western Pacific, where Japanese studies have suggested the catch may be approaching its upper sustainable limit.

Gulland (1970) and Fullenbaum (1970) provide some specific estimates of the potential yield, by ocean, of the principal tuna species. Their estimates are summarized in table 10. Fullenbaum's estimates for the Pacific and Indian oceans are considerably higher than those by Gulland. For the Atlantic, Fullenbaum's estimate is lower than Gulland's. It appears that much of the difference is related to the estimates of skipjack potential. In addition, Fullenbaum does not consider bigeye in the Atlantic. Fullenbaum's estimate of 2,330,000 metric tons for the major market species falls slightly above the upper limit of Gulland's estimated range of 1,560,000–2,250,000.

Fullenbaum's estimate of skipjack yield in the Pacific and Indian oceans is probably too high. For example, the total skipjack population for the Indian Ocean has been estimated at 300,000–400,000 metric tons by Kikawa *et al.* (1969). The maxi-

Table 10. Estimated Potential Catches of Tuna from the World Oceans

(000 metric tons)

Region	Estimated maximum average sustainable yield	
	Fullenbaum	Gulland
Atlantic Ocean		
Albacore	40.4 ⎫	
Yellowfin	44.4 ⎬	200–250
Bluefin	18.8 ⎭	
Skipjack	101.1	250–300
Total Atlantic	204.7	450–550
Pacific Ocean		
Albacore	133.2 ⎫	
Yellowfin	205.4 ⎬	350–450
Bluefin	72.7 ⎬	
Bigeye	109.6 ⎭	
Skipjack	1,080.0	500–800
Total Pacific	1,600.9	850–1,250
Indian Ocean		
Large tunas	265.9	160–300
Skipjack	258.9	100–150
Total Indian	524.8	260–450
Total all oceans	2,330.0	1,560–2,250
Bonitos and little tuna (all oceans)	240.0	500
World totals	2,570.0	2,060–2,750

Sources: Fullenbaum (1970, table 14, p. 42). Gulland (1970, table p. 4).

mum average sustainable yield would reasonably be somewhat less than 50 percent of this, or more in the range estimated by Gulland. Further, as was stated earlier, Japanese studies indicate that the skipjack resource in the western Pacific may be approaching its maximum. This indicates that the total Pacific potential is most likely lower than that suggested by Fullenbaum.

Table 11 compares Joseph's 1971 estimated catch (Joseph, 1973) with the estimated potential catch by Gulland and Fullenbaum. Selecting as an example the midpoint of Gulland's estimate, i.e., 1,900,000 metric tons, and comparing it with the 1971 estimated catch of 1,213,000 metric tons, the data suggest that the 1971 catch of the major market species of tuna may be in

Table 11. World Catch of Major Market Species of Tuna and Estimated Maximum Sustained Yield

(000 metric tons)

Source	Atlantic Ocean	Indian Ocean	Pacific Ocean	Total
Joseph (1973)				
Estimated 1971 catch	295	163	755	1,213
Fullenbaum (1970)				
Estimated maximum potential[a]	205	525	1,600	2,330
Gulland (1970)				
Estimated maximum potential[b]	450–550	260–450	850–1,250	1,560–2,250

[a] Excluding estimates for bonitos.
[b] Excluding estimates for frigate mackerel and little tunas.

the general range of 70 percent of the maximum sustained yield of these species.

FUTURE DEMAND FOR THE MAJOR TUNA SPECIES

The world production and consumption of tuna has been increasing at an annual rate of about 8 percent during the past 20 years (Joseph, 1973). It seems logical to expect that if adequate supplies of tuna were available, consumption would continue to increase. Bell (1969) projected the world consumption of tuna to 1990. This is summarized in table 12 under assumptions of unlimited supplies and constant prices. Recognizing that it is not realistic to consider that prices would remain constant, Bell went on to project consumption under an assumption that price would double by 1990. The latter estimate, however, may not be as useful as that in table 12 because an implicit assumption in the latter estimate is that tuna prices would double relative to all other food prices.

As the various tuna stocks approach full exploitation, catch per unit of effort declines, cost per pound landed increases, and prices rise significantly. However, at the same time there will be upward pressures on the prices of meat, poultry, and other fish products. Thus, as long as prices of other protein sources increase at approximately the same rate as tuna prices, table 12 can be considered as a general guide to the growth in the demand for tuna. Certainly the potential increase in demand is adequate to

Table 12. Forecasts of Total World Tuna Consumption to 1990, Based on Increases in Population and Per Capita Income for Selected Countries[a]

(round weight, 000 metric tons)

Country	1966 actual	1970	1975	1980	1985	1990
United States	382.8	511.3	671.6	845.3	1,055.8	1,318.4
Japan	378.8	408.6	514.5	649.5	820.3	1,037.2
EEC	159.0	210.5	281.4	382.8	552.5	713.4
Spain	69.6	69.4	72.4	97.5	133.1	183.7
Peru	50.2	98.7	137.3	194.7	275.1	387.4
Taiwan	44.8	47.9	71.8	119.7	217.0	425.0
Turkey	16.0	17.9	20.6	23.5	26.9	30.7
Canada	9.7	11.6	15.2	19.5	25.0	32.1
United Kingdom	7.6	7.4	7.8	8.0	8.3	8.6
Total, selected countries	1,118.5	1,383.3	1,792.6	2,340.5	3,084.0	4,136.5
Grand total (projected at 120% of total for selected countries)	1,320.0	1,659.6	2,151.1	2,808.6	3,700.8	4,963.8

Source: Bell (1969).

[a] Prices are held constant at 1966 value, as if unlimited supplies were available. These projections include all tuna and tunalike species—not just the six major species.

bring pressure on tuna stocks up to the maximum sustainable yield levels estimated by Gulland and Fullenbaum within the next 10–20 years—and possibly even sooner. For example, in table 12 Bell estimates the total world consumption in 1980 at 2,808,600 metric tons. Joseph (1973) indicates that the six major species usually account for about 65 percent of the total catch of all tuna and tunalike species. Sixty-five percent of Bell's 1980 total demand estimate would be about 1,900,000 metric tons—or approximately the midpoint of Gulland's maximum average sustainable yield estimate for the major tuna species (table 11).

In an attempt to examine the time trend in the catch of tuna and tunalike species, the authors used regression analysis.[1] In this model C is total catch in thousands of metric tons and T is time,

[1] Several linear and curvilinear models were tested but it was found that the linear model of the form $C = a + bT$ gave the best fit to the historical data used in the analysis.

with 1952 − 1. Using catch data for the period 1952−70 the following equation was derived:

$$C = 609.4 + 58.8T$$

The measure of closeness of fit (r) was 0.977 where 1.0 would be a perfect fit of all the data points on the regression line. This equation shows that over the period the catch of tuna and tunalike species went up about 58.8 thousand metric tons each year.

Assuming this trend continues, this equation predicts that the midpoint (2,405,000 metric tons) of Gulland's range of estimated maximum average sustainable yield for tuna and tunalike species will be reached in the early 1980s.[2] Considering that the maximum sustainable yield levels for the major market species will probably be reached before that for the little tunas, this simple trend analysis gives further weight to the argument that the maximum average sustainable yield levels for all major tuna species will be reached within only a few years.

Summary

The available evidence indicates that the oceans cannot yield much more than a 25 to 35 percent increase in the catch of the six major market species of tuna. Based on projections of income and population increases in the major tuna-consuming nations, it appears that past increases in demand for tuna will continue and that this increasing demand will tend to bring the fishing effort for these species to the maximum average sustainable yield level during the next decade.

[2] Note that the midpoint of Gulland's estimate (2,405,000 metric tons) is within 165,000 metric tons of Fullenbaum's estimate.

V Implications of Alternative Management Schemes

THE PREVIOUS CHAPTERS have described a situation in which the fishing effort on five of the six major market species of tuna is at or near the maximum average sustainable yield levels. Although there appears to be a potential for expanded skipjack catches, increasing demand and the resultant increase in fishing effort are expected to soon bring this species to its maximum average yield.

Joseph (1973, figure 4) indicates that rapid growth has occurred in the world tuna fleet capacity. He shows that in 1964 total capacity increased (primarily due to large additions by the Republic of Korea and Taiwan) by 25 percent over the 1963 capacity. From 1964 to 1971 total fleet capacity increased by about 46 percent—an average of almost 7 percent annually. Joseph projected a 12 percent increase from 1971 to 1974, representing an estimated average annual increase of about 4 percent. If the growth rate from 1974 to 1984 averages just 3 percent annually, the total world capacity by 1984 would be at or above that necessary to harvest the maximum sustainable yield of all species. This projection is consistent with the simple linear projection of total catch by the authors reported in chapter IV.

It seems evident that the extensive migrations of tunas, the increased mobility of the tuna fishing fleets, and the rapid expansion of capacity in these fleets combine to present serious and immediate global management problems. Unless rational management agreements are reached soon, competition for the international tuna markets will intensify competition for the tuna resources. The result will be excess fishing effort and significant losses to the world community because of declining yields and unnecessarily high catching costs.

It must be recognized that without proper management arrangements for the six major species there is a real danger of overfishing the tuna stocks. This could lead to regional depletion of some stocks, with severe effects on the future potential wealth that could be obtained from these resources. This is certain to bring about attempts to acquire exclusive rights to the resources—either by unilateral extension of fishing jurisdictions (possibly beyond 200 miles) or by multilateral exclusive arrangements. Therefore, the consequences of continued open access to these common property resources will, as described by Christy (1973), be biologic and economic waste and an increase in the severity of conflicts related to the use of tuna resources. This brings to the world community the necessity of immediately dealing with the problems of tuna resource management and wealth distribution. (See Christy, 1973, for a detailed discussion of the importance of recognizing the distinction between production and distribution decisions.)

OBJECTIVES OF MANAGEMENT

A joint meeting of the Indo-Pacific Fisheries Council and the Indian Ocean Fishery Commission resulted in the publication of certain objectives of tuna management (FAO, 1971). These included:

1. Maintenance of tuna stocks at levels that provide high sustained yields.
2. Conservation measures that do not interfere with development of unexploited stocks.
3. Measures which afford the opportunity for countries not yet participating in tuna fishing to build up their fishing industries.

The authors of this report agree with these objectives but believe that a rational management plan must also specifically allow for:

4. Improved economic efficiency, and
5. Appropriate distribution of the benefits.

With respect to objective 1, it is important to note that, as described earlier, certain of the major species in some areas are already exploited at a level beyond the maximum average sustainable yield. Also, it is important to recognize the interrelationship among these objectives. That is, an attempt to meet objective 3 (allowing new entrants) could conflict with objective 1. Therefore, objectives 1 and 3 must be considered together and related to objective 5, appropriate distribution of benefits.

Further, the objective of improved economic efficiency in the tuna fisheries cannot be attained if objective 1 is met solely through overall catch quotas. As will be discussed in more detail later, overall quotas ultimately lead to excess capitalization. The attainment of improved economic efficiency must also facilitate adjustments to changes in comparative advantage among nations in tuna harvesting or processing by allowing for shifts from high-cost nations to those with lower labor and capital costs. This

37

implies that catching rights should be marketable or at least transferable among nations.

It is possible that emphasizing economic efficiency could conflict with desires to provide employment opportunities. However, the protection of labor opportunities (which could be one aspect under objective 5) may not be as important in tuna fishing as in coastal fishing because of the generally high mobility of those employed in tuna fishing.

Recognizing these interrelationships and potential conflicts, however, the above five objectives provide a basis for determining the implications of alternative management schemes.

PRESENT MANAGEMENT ARRANGEMENTS

Many nations have been concerned about the increasing pressures on certain tuna stocks. This has resulted in the establishment of regional bodies which have attempted to develop programs for the management of tuna stocks. Joseph (1973) provides an overview of the four regional management bodies that now exist. The oldest is the Inter-American Tropical Tuna Commission (IATTC), which was established by a treaty between Costa Rica and the United States in 1949. The IATTC became operational in 1951 and has been actively operating in the eastern Pacific region since that time. A summary of the IATTC development, regional regulations for management, and their economic and political implications has been given by Joseph (1970). The IATTC is the only regional fisheries management body which has an internationally recruited scientific staff for promulgating management regulations.

In 1969 an International Commission for the Conservation of Atlantic Tunas (ICCAT) was established for the eastern tropical Atlantic Ocean. The ICCAT convention now covers all waters of the Atlantic Ocean, including the adjacent seas. Attempts to meet convention objectives are being made by appointing panels for the different species. The ICCAT staff consists only of a secretariat with no scientific research group. The IATTC and ICCAT are independent commissions established by separate international treaties.

The other two bodies concerned with tuna conservation are the Indian Ocean Fishery Commission (IOFC) and the Indo-Pacific Fisheries Council (IPFC), both established by the Food and Agriculture Organization of the United Nations (FAO). Neither the IOFC nor the IPFC has a research staff of its own but relies on supporting bodies and outside help. The area of concern of the IPFC includes the marine and freshwaters of the Indo-Pacific region. IPFC has established a committee on tuna management in the Indo-Pacific region. The IPFC and IOFC have sponsored *ad hoc* meetings of scientists to study the tuna situation (see, for example, FAO, 1971a).

The IATTC has taken some important resource conservation steps by setting annual catch quotas for yellowfin tuna in the eastern tropical Pacific. Although the commission has been successful in maintaining the yield from the yellowfin resource, many problems have developed as a result of this type of regulation. Joseph (1973, pp. 14–15) outlines some of the complexities as follows:

> Since 1966 the fishery in the eastern Pacific has changed remarkably. . . . The fleet has increased nearly three times. . . . competition has increased sharply and the open season for yellowfin fishing has decreased from about ten months to less than three. Developing nations maintain that under the present management system their tunas fisheries cannot develop, and there are strong pressures for increased special allocations. As these allocations are established there is beginning to be a shift of flag vessels from the nations with large fleets to the nations with small fleets. Each nation with vessels fishing in the CYRA is responsible for establishing and enforcing its own tuna regulations based on the recommendations of the IATTC. As the vessels relocate themselves in other countries the number of nations involved in the fishery increases, along with the problems of implementation and enforcement.

Although the statement by Joseph indicates the problems facing this group, he does not mention explicitly the major difficulty associated with the total catch quota approach taken by the commission—overcapitalization and economic waste. A total catch quota without additional regulations, such as national quotas or limitations on entry, generates economic waste through overcapitalization in the "race" to harvest as much of the resource as possible before the catch limit is reached. Indicative of this is the fact that the yellowfin open season is now less than 3 months long. Table 13 and figure 7 illustrate the trend in carrying capacity in the regulated area.[1]

In addition to the economic waste generated in this fishery,

---

[1] Changes in carrying capacity provide a general indication of changes in fishing capacity.

Table 13 A. Surface Fishing Fleets Operating in IATTC Yellowfin Regulations Area, by Year

Year	Total no. of vessels	Total carrying capacity (short tons)	Purse seine of total capacity (%)	U.S. flag of total capacity (%)
1962	236	40,553	78.3	90.1
1963	251	44,913	86.4	89.8
1964	252	45,661	88.0	88.7
1965	253	46,743	87.5	89.9
1966	245	46,096	86.2	88.0
1967	239	45,973	86.9	89.9
1968	249	57,787	89.0	80.4
1969	250	62,219	90.6	85.4
1970	270	72,613	91.4	82.8
1971	352	95,035	92.3	79.0
1972	373	115,737	92.4	76.7
Estimated active through April 1973	272	126,429	95.5	75.5
Estimated for 1973	353	133,055	94.3	72.5
Estimated range early 1974	378–393	150,806–161,506	94.8–95.2	72.3–67.5

Table 13B. Estimated Fleet Active in Area, January–April 1973

Flag	No. of vessels	Gear	Total carrying capacity (short tons)
Bermuda	2	Seiner	612
Canada	7	Seiner	5,250
Costa Rica	4	Seiner	1,019
Ecuador	10	Seiner	1,398
Ecuador	22	Bolichero and bait boat	675
France	3	Seiner	4,353
Mexico	16	15 seiner and 1 bait boat	6,067
Panama	5	Seiner	2,721
Peru	5	Seiner	955
Spain	5	Seiner	5,543
Japan and Netherlands	2	Seiner	2,350
United States	131	Seiner	90,614
United States	37	Bait boat	4,291
United States	23	Jig	581

Source: IATTC unpublished information.

40

Figure 7. Growth in carrying capacity of surface fleets in IATTC yellowfin regulation area.

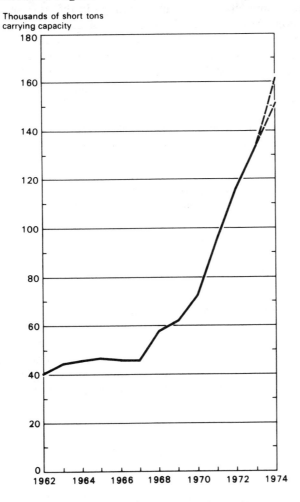

Thousands of short tons
carrying capacity

there is another problem associated with the IATTC approach. As was indicated in chapter II, when the yellowfin catch limit is reached, these vessels begin to operate in other areas or fish for other tuna species, many of which are near or at maximum sustainable yield levels. Thus, while this approach may satisfy the objective of maintaining high sustained yield of yellowfin in regulated areas, it does not meet other objectives set out above.

In spite of the attempts of existing management bodies, such as IATTC, IOFC, IFPC, and ICCAT, there has been little

41

progress toward rational worldwide tuna management programs. It is clear that improved and coordinated management approaches are needed. Some alternatives are examined in the next section.

Before considering these alternatives and examining how well they satisfy the objectives set out above, it is useful to reiterate certain important points brought out earlier in this report. First, with tuna as with most fish resources, the concept of benefits to be gained may differ substantially among states. These benefits include but are not limited to:

Income and employment gained in harvesting tuna.

Income and employment gained in processing or transshipping tuna products.

A source of protein as a consumption item.

Foreign exchange gained through the export market.

Possible payments or rent to be gained through licenses or taxes.

A trade-off item through which to obtain benefits in areas such as concessions relative to international trade of other products; access to marine minerals, military objectives, or other fish species.

Second, the nature of world demand and international trade for tuna products dictates that tuna will be consumed primarily in the higher income nations. Thus, distribution of the benefits from tuna resources among developing nations probably cannot include substantial consumption of tuna in these nations. Rather, the developing countries should look principally toward sharing in the income and employment at the harvesting, processing, and international trade levels or by extracting revenues from the users.

Third, there will soon be adequate fleet capacity among the nations now actively fishing for tuna to harvest the maximum average sustainable yield of the major tuna stocks. Additions to the world tuna fleets during the next decade will not result in greater catches than the current or slightly expanded fleets can produce. Effective management, therefore, requires that, if there is to be provision for nations to enter the fisheries for the major tuna species, methods must be developed which allow for transferring effort from existing fishing nations to the new nations.

Fourth, the processing segment of the world tuna industry is probably more concerned about obtaining a stable supply of good quality tuna at the lowest possible cost than about which nation or nations own the fishing vessels. The processing firms are in general well financed and efficient. Recent developments in Latin

America, American Samoa, and other developing nations are evidence that these firms are willing to establish operations in areas where the source of tuna is cheapest, and transportation, import taxes, or other restrictions do not constrain effective competition in the international tuna market.

Fifth, the natural distribution and migratory behavior of the tuna stocks relative to limits of national jurisdiction complicate the decisions relating to management of the stocks and wealth distribution.

These points should be kept in mind as alternative management strategies are considered.

ALTERNATIVE MANAGEMENT ARRANGEMENTS

It is emphasized that a full listing and evaluation of all possible management arrangements would require inputs of time and funds well beyond those available to the authors of this study. Therefore, the alternatives contained in this section should not be considered as exhaustive. Further, the implications drawn regarding those alternatives should be considered as general. They are largely intended to provide guidelines for further in-depth analyses of the alternative approaches and their effects.

Numerous regulatory techniques have been proposed as methods of limiting catch and effort and/or distributing the benefits from world tuna resources. These include overall catch quotas, national quotas, direct effort limitations, licensing, and taxation. Also, various institutional arrangements for carrying out these techniques have been advanced. Examples are extended coastal state jurisdiction or economic zones, regional coastal authorities, regional high seas commissions, and a global management agency.

Although certain of these may be effective in maintaining high sustainable yields or even enhancing economic efficiency, no one technique or institutional approach automatically attains all five of the objectives mentioned at the outset of this chapter. This is especially true of the objective related to appropriate distribution of the benefits from world tuna resources.

To address this latter objective, consideration must be given to the relative claims of developing states, landlocked and coastal states, states that rely heavily on tuna as a consumption item, states that already have significant investment of labor and capital in the tuna industry, and those states that wish to develop their tuna harvesting or processing capabilities. Certainly an answer to this complex question will not be forthcoming in this paper. But the issue must be faced if progress is to be made in developing rational tuna management approaches. Also, no approach automatically answers the question of at what level catch or effort should be limited. That is, should catch be maintained at the maximum average sustainable yield level or should effort be maintained at some level below this, such as at the maximum economic efficiency level? (See Christy, 1973, for an elaboration of this latter point.)

An appropriate management scheme for tuna must include regulatory techniques designed to meet the objectives of management identified above and an effective institutional arrangement for carrying out these techniques. The following discussion first presents some alternative regulatory techniques and their implications. Then, certain alternative institutional arrangements are outlined and their effectiveness for managing the tuna resources of the oceans is evaluated.

Alternative Regulatory Techniques

Overall Catch Quotas. It seems appropriate to dismiss overall quotas as a sole technique in that it encourages economic waste. While this may be an effective short-term method to prevent immediate overexploitation of a fish population, the waste generated through overcapitalization in the race to catch as much as possible before the quota is reached (as exemplified by the previous discussions relating to the IATTC) precludes this technique from consideration as a viable or acceptable long-term approach by the world community. A total quota approach also would have important distributional implications. It would generally enforce the distributional pattern that now exists and the catch would go to those states that currently have the available capital to invest most rapidly. This would probably tend to restrict the tuna catch primarily to those countries currently involved in tuna harvesting. Further, unless the openings of the seasons for species in each area were closely coordinated, this approach would be an artificial determinant of fishing costs. That is, heavy fishing on certain species or in certain areas would be determined by when the season is open rather than when costs of catching are lowest. Although a total quota system might be relatively easy to agree upon as a short-term interim solution, the fact that it will allow further buildup of fishing effort will probably make longer term national solutions more difficult to bring about.

National Quotas. This technique can offer considerable improvement over the previous one. Under this approach the total

44

permissible yield would be determined and then divided among the relevant nations. They would be given national quotas which they would agree not to exceed. These quotas could be set by species and/or by area. Theoretically, this approach would permit each state to adopt whatever objective it chooses, such as maximum employment or maximum economic efficiency.

There are other important factors that must be examined. An overall catch limitation for each tuna species in each area, subdivided among nations, could effectively maintain a high sustainable yield and at the same time prevent economically wasteful competition among the states. It would not, however, prevent intrastate competition. Without intrastate restrictions this would tend to lead to overcapitalization of effort within each state as individuals attempted to capture as much of their own state's quota as possible before this quota was reached. If some states attempted to prevent this intrastate overexpansion of effort while others did not, the individuals fishing under controls of those states limiting effort would actually lose. This could result from higher costs imposed on individuals in the states limiting effort by those in states not limiting effort. An example of this would be the relatively large amount of effort that could be exerted in certain areas or seasons of high abundance by those fleets which were allowed to build up.

Other important questions raised by this approach include how to initially distribute the quotas among nations; how to allow for new entrants to the fishery; and how to distribute the benefits among states other than those actively engaged in the fishery. If national quotas for tuna were based only on historical catch, the number of states sharing in the major part of the benefits would be quite limited (see table 1). Additionally, proximity, which may be a useful criterion for allocating quotas for certain coastal species, does not seem to be an appropriate sole criterion for allocating the quota or benefits from highly migratory species such as tunas.

If national quotas are established, it is important that these quotas be marketable. This would help to assure that the quotas are available to the most efficient or lowest cost producers. It is possible, for example, that Korea or Taiwan might wish to purchase part of the U.S. or Japanese national quota in view of their lower labor and capital costs. Allowing for the transfer of quotas among nations would also help to solve the problem of how to allow for new entrants to the fishery.

This system does have some flexibility with respect to the distribution objective. For example, quotas could be allocated to

45

nonfishing coastal states. These states could then extract some benefit from the resource—by leasing the right to exploit that quota to a fishing nation—without having to invest their own labor and capital, which might be better used elsewhere. The problem of how to allocate benefits among landlocked states, however, cannot be solved unless some form of licensing or taxation is involved. This is discussed below.

Direct Effort Limitations. Through direct effort limitations a determination would be made of the allowable catch by species or area, and then an estimate of the number of standardized units of effort necessary to take this catch would be made. The total allowable effort would then be allocated among the fishing states.

This technique could overcome the economic waste from overcapitalization that would result from national and overall catch quotas. Implicit in this approach, however, are the same basic problems discussed under national quotas. The questions of how the effort is allocated among states, how to allow for new entrants, and how, if at all, the benefits can be shared by non−tuna fishing states have to be answered.

There are additional complex issues involved with this technique. In tuna fishery, different types of fishing methods are used—principally longlining, purse seining, and bait fishing. To effectively restrict effort, a standardized method of measuring effort would have to be developed and applied against each vessel in the fishery. Also, adjustments would have to be made for changes in fishing effectiveness, such as improved search or spotting methods. Rothschild (1972) and others have addressed the problem of definition of fishing effort, but the solution in regard to tuna fishing has not yet been reached.

One potentially serious shortcoming of direct effort restrictions is that they may tend to retard technological advancements. If technological improvements are made, the management agency, in its attempt to keep effective effort at a given level, would have to reduce the allowed effort, with a possibility of no real gain to the vessel owners. For example, if a technique that increased harvesting effectiveness by 10 percent were adopted by all vessel owners, the management agency would have to cut back proportionally on the amount of time the vessels could fish. This would be necessary to maintain the desired catch level. The owners would then have to leave their vessels idle for a portion of the time or search for alternative species, which may be available only at increased costs. This, of course, clearly illustrates the complexity of the tuna management problem and shows that it is

46

not logical to initiate regulation for certain areas without taking into account the effects on these or other areas.

Christy (1973, chapter 2) provides a more detailed discussion of the advantages and disadvantages associated with restrictions on direct fishing effort. However, considering the complexities involved in attempting to regulate the world tuna fisheries by this technique, this approach seems less desirable than the national quota technique discussed previously.

License Fees and Taxation. None of the above techniques directly provides for appropriating from the tuna fisheries revenue or rent which could be used for financing the management agency, for payment to coastal states for allowing fishing in their jurisdictional waters, and/or for distribution to non–tuna fishing states.

License fees or taxation can be used to appropriate revenue for these purposes while at the same time serving as a means for controlling the catch of a particular species. For example, license fees or landings taxes, if set high enough, could artifically raise the cost of harvesting to a point where additional fishing effort would not be profitable. Then, by requiring each vessel to pay an appropriate fee either through (1) a license fee based on vessel size, (2) a license fee that allows for landing a certain amount of fish, or (3) a direct tax on landings, the management agency or the coastal state could limit catch, because those unwilling to pay the fee would not enter the fishery. An example of this technique is the license fee charged by the Japanese government, described by Asada (1972) and referred to in chapter I of this report.

It is important to note that the collection of a tax or license fee will not result in an increase in world tuna prices. Rather, this is a method for extracting rent that would accrue to individual vessel operators if fishing effort were limited, or for extracting revenue that would be dissipated in the form of higher costs due to overcapitalization if effort were not limited.

While this method has the advantage of providing a means of collecting revenue as well as a means of controlling catch, some very basic but complex questions must be considered. These include: (1) Who issues the license and collects the fee (i.e., a central management agency, individual coastal states, or some combination of these)? (2) How are the licenses to be allocated among fishing states? (3) Who will share in the revenue that is collected?

It is important that any license fee or taxation approach be closely coordinated or determined by a single agency (even if the fees are to be collected by the coastal states) and that the fees be applied wherever the stock is caught—within or beyond national jurisdictions. The reason for this is that the license fee approach, if adopted, should be used for controlling catch at a rational level, as indicated in the first objective mentioned previously. If left to individual coastal states, each state might attempt to attract more and more effort (and thus license or tax revenue) into its jurisdiction by lowering the rate. This could result in the rate being too low to effectively control catch. In other words, there would be a danger that because the tuna species do not remain in the jurisdictional waters of the coastal states, certain states could become more interested in generating short-term revenue than in conserving the stocks.

One method of allocating licenses among fishing states—an alternative that has important implications for economic efficiency—is to auction a limited number of licenses to the highest bidders. Those individuals, or states if the case may be, who could make the greatest gain from holding the licenses would tend to bid the highest.

This approach might have the disadvantage of keeping out of the fishery certain nations that are just developing their fishing capabilities and thus may not be able to pay high prices for the licenses. However, helping to subsidize new fishing nations could be one alternative use of the revenue generated, provided this did not simply add to an already existing excess effort.

In any effort to appropriate revenues from the world tuna fisheries, it is important to recognize that the amount of revenue is limited. For example, it was indicated previously that the 1970 exvessel value of the world tuna fisheries was about 632 million dollars (U.S.). Allowing for an increase in value since 1970, it is probably safe to assume that the present value is in the range of 650 million dollars (U.S.). If, for example, 10 percent of this could be appropriated through a tax or license system, the revenue available for distribution would be 65 million dollars. It is logical that a portion of this appropriated revenue would be used to finance the required tuna research, statistics collection, enforcement, and general operations of the tuna management agency (or agencies). This, on a worldwide scale, would probably take several million dollars, leaving an amount substantially less than 65 million dollars for distribution. If, as a further example, this were distributed equally among all nations, each nation would receive less than half of one million dollars annually. This serves to point out that the world tuna fisheries cannot provide exceedingly large economic rents to the world community and still allow the states involved in tuna fishing to obtain acceptable economic returns.

On the other hand, it must be recognized that any economic rent that can be collected by the world community is better than allowing unmanaged tuna fishing—a situation in which all will eventually lose because of declining yields and unnecessarily high harvesting costs. While it is important to be cognizant of the constraints and implications of the regulatory techniques described above, it is likewise important to recognize that appropriate and acceptable regulation must be established to prevent depletion of tuna stocks and worldwide economic waste in the tuna fisheries. Therefore, although the above discussions show that it is likely no single technique can meet all of the objectives of management identified at the beginning of this chapter, it is clear that certain combinations of these could satisfy the objectives. For example, national quotas along with a tax system and allowance for transfer of quotas could meet all of these objectives.

The following section outlines certain institutional arrangements that might be established to carry out the regulatory techniques described above.

Institutional Arrangements

Coastal and Regional Economic Zones. There is reason to believe that the outcome of the UN-sponsored Law of the Sea Conference will be the advocation of some form of extended marine fisheries jurisdiction. An increasing interest has been shown on the part of many countries in some form of economic zone or patrimonial sea, whereby national fisheries jurisdiction becomes extended well offshore—for example, to 200 miles, to the edge of the continental shelf, to a depth of 200 meters, or some other designated area.

If extended fisheries jurisdiction over the waters of the continental shelf—say to 200 miles—is accepted by the conference and no allowance is made for foreign fishing within these zones, the opportunities for nations engaged in surface fisheries, such as Spain, France, and the United States, would certainly be reduced. It is expected, for example, that the U.S. catch of tuna would drop initially. The initiation of a 200-mile limit by Mexico would essentially eliminate the U.S. bait-boat fleet operating in the IATTC regions. The U.S. bait-boat fleet must rely on live bait sources close to the shore. Much of the bait is caught off the Mexican coast. Also, bait boats do not have the range of the larger purse seiners and, regardless of the live bait source, could not effectively operate at distances beyond the 200-mile limit. The French and Spanish fisheries in the northeast Atlantic and the developing French purse seine fishery in the Caribbean would likewise be significantly affected. Additionally, any of the longline or surface fisheries that now exist around the Pacific islands and in much of the Indian Ocean would have to move further offshore and likely incur more costs.

It is generally recognized, however, that as the size of tuna fishing vessels has increased, so has the proportion of the total catch of tuna and tunalike fishes caught beyond 200 miles from land. Recent statistics compiled by IATTC for the eastern tropical Pacific Ocean show that for vessels over 400 tons in capacity size, approximately 50 percent of the yellowfin catch and 30 percent of the skipjack catch are being taken outside 200 miles. In the case of vessels under 200 tons in capacity, the share of the catch outside the 200-mile limit is only 8 percent for yellowfin and 2 percent for skipjack.

Felando (1972) indicated that a limited number of large U.S. superseiners could survive and do fairly well if excluded from the 200-mile zone of the eastern tropical Pacific Ocean. The generally deeper location of the thermocline in the Indian Ocean and the concentration of fishing effort on or near continental shelves in the Atlantic Ocean suggest that surface fishing with large purse seines probably would be less successful for the major market species of tuna in these areas if large purse seiners were excluded from the 200-mile zone. The longline fishery would be less affected than surface fisheries in all areas because, as was pointed out earlier in this report, it is carried out over extremely large areas in all oceans. The other forms of surface fishing, which include pole and line or trolling, could be significantly affected. However, the current size of the catch by these methods and the numbers of vessels using these methods in the waters of other coastal states seem to be relatively small.

It is important to note that significant technological improvements in the ability to locate and catch tuna through various forms of remote sensing devices could substantially alter the consequences of extended marine fisheries jurisdiction. Remote sensing from aerospace platforms may provide more effective means for locating tuna and tunalike fish resources and predicting their distribution both spatially and temporally.[2] This type of development could minimize the effects of coastal state exclusive jurisdiction by permitting effective capture techniques outside zones of exclusive jurisdiction.

We recognize that the type of exclusive jurisdiction described above, in which there is an absolute prohibition on foreign fishing within economic zones, is not likely to result. Most states would find it to their advantage to extract revenues or other benefits from foreign fishermen rather than to prohibit access to resources they are not fully utilizing.

A more probable alternative is that the coastal states, rather than excluding any foreign fishing activity, would allow regulated foreign fishing activity. The regulations will likely involve some form of licensing, leasing, or taxation. This could give the coastal states not involved in tuna fishing, or states with fleets that cannot effectively compete with those of the major fishing nations, a source of economic rent from the resources within their economic zones. This alternative would not require that the coastal state develop its own fleet in order to participate in the distribution of the benefits from resources along its coast. This could then allow the coastal state to utilize its scarce investment capital, along with the revenue obtained from foreign fishing activities, in ventures with relatively greater returns than could be obtained in the high-cost, intensively competitive tuna fisheries.

The coastal state or regional authority would have to use care not to price itself out of the market. It was pointed out earlier that the major tuna fleets, with some added costs, can take most of the maximum average sustainable yield of each of the major

[2] Much has been written on the distribution and migration of tuna as affected by various environmental stimuli. Nakamura (1969) has summarized much of this information and has hypothesized that tuna habitats consist of an ocean current or water masses and that tuna migration could be separated into migration within and between habitats. Hela and Laevastu (1970) have also reported that fish search for and select a certain optimum combination of physical and biological conditions in the environment. Mooveover, Pearcy (1971) has indicated that factors presently used by fishermen to locate albacore, such as sea surface temperature, water color, fronts and location of other vessels, are amenable to remote sensing. Nearly synoptic representations of large areas can be provided by remote sensing, and repeated surveys of a given area can illustrate the dynamics of detectable ocean features. In general, it is clear that the present state of the art in remote sensor technology is rapidly changing, and there is a possibility that future data will provide valuable information on large-scale phenomena of significance to tuna fisheries.

species outside an economic zone such as a 200-mile limit. Thus, if the license fee charged by the coastal state were greater than the added cost of fishing outside the zone, the major fleets would simply move outside the economic zones and the coastal states would not receive a share of the benefits. This would be disadvantageous to everyone—the coastal states, the fishing states, and the world community. It should also be noted that the coastal states should take care that they restrict the foreign fishing effort directly—through limits or appropriate tax rates. Complicated "bureaucratic" procedures as a method of limiting licenses are wasteful to all.

Additional important possibilities under this alternative would be the encouragement by the coastal states of joint ventures or the use of their ports and facilities for vessel bases, transshipping, or processing. As pointed out earlier in this paper, Japan and the United States have already initiated these procedures with several developing states. Such agreements would allow for gains to the coastal states in terms of employment and income generated within their economy. This approach would, of course, carry with it any advantages or disadvantages of foreign investment in a developing country. It could, however, provide significant economic benefits to the coastal states without their having to develop fishing fleets to compete with efficient foreign fleets that already essentially have the capability of exerting the maximum sustainable yield levels of effort.

While this alternative may have the advantage of allowing for distribution of benefits among more states, it is not sufficient to handle effectively the problems of managing the tuna stocks.

Considering the five objectives specified earlier in this chapter, an economic zone approach without some form of international control would leave much to be desired. The major market species are highly migratory and continually move in and out of the 200-mile or similar line. Any attempt, therefore, to manage these species solely through the initiation of a 200-mile fishing limit or economic zone cannot be successful from the point of view of conservation or management. Effective management and distribution of benefits for the tuna resources of the oceans require authority over the high seas as well as over near coastal waters. For example, fees for fishing on the high seas would have to be charged and coordinated with those charged by the coastal states. Thus, an economic zone approach combined with high seas management agencies offers an alternative that should be seriously considered by the world community. This is discussed in a later section.

Regional High Seas Commissions. Considering the shortcomings inherent in the above-described economic zone approach, it is possible that the existing commissions in the Atlantic, Indian, and Pacific oceans could be utilized as the nucleus of an appropriate management arrangement. To be effective, the present commissions would have to be substantially strengthened and expanded. Regional (oceanwide) commissions could be designed to operate in conjunction with narrow coastal state jurisdictions or with expanded jurisdictions as described in the previous section.

If the arrangement included only narrow (i.e., 3 or 12 miles) coastal state jurisdiction, some special consideration would have to be given to coastal state interests.

On the other hand, if the arrangement were one that included expanded coastal jurisdiction, the regional agencies should be given the power to regulate and effectively limit the fishing effort within the coastal jurisdiction as well as on the high seas. This could include the power to set overall quotas, and possibly the power to determine national quotas and to tax or issue licenses. It is clear that it would not be desirable to have regional commissions with responsibility only outside jurisdictional waters—200 miles, for example. The result of such an approach could be conflict and competition among the coastal states, as described in the previous section, as well as conflict between the coastal states and the commission. Therefore, while an approach that would allow separate responsibilities and control by coastal states out to some artificial line and then commission responsibility and control beyond that line might be a relatively easy direction for the decision makers at the Law of the Sea Conference to take, it is not an acceptable direction if the desire is to reduce potential conflict and to move toward fulfilling the five objectives set out earlier in this chapter.

A further consideration under the alternative of regional commissions is that the regulations and activities of these regional agencies would have to be closely coordinated. This would include research and statistics-gathering programs (see Joseph, 1973). In addition, coordinated activities would be essential because of the highly mobile nature of the tuna fleets. The relative shift in effort from the Pacific to the Atlantic Ocean at the end of the open yellowfin season in the IATTC-regulated area is evidence of the need for coordination. Further, it is crucial that the regulations be set so that fishing in each ocean and on each species, as far as is practical, would be allowed at the times of the year when harvesting costs are lowest.

The implications of this are that certain global guidelines and regulations are needed for coordination. Therefore, a management alternative that would include regional commissions, each acting totally independently of the others, would not provide an effective approach to world tuna management. Rather, it is important to develop an institutional arrangement that allows for certain global management decisions.

Global Management Agency. A single worldwide management agency would be an effective arrangement for dealing with highly migratory species such as the major tuna species. This agency could determine the appropriate amount of effort or catch for each species, issue licenses or collect taxes, and distribute the rent. Theoretically, such an agency could manage the world tuna resources in a manner that would maximize the amount of revenue or economic rent for the world community. It is questionable, however, whether such an agency, with the powers implied by the above role, could be set up in time to prevent excessive additions to the world tuna fleets. As pointed out by Gulland (1972), such an agency would require extensive organizational efforts by the world community.

CONCLUSIONS

Without an effective worldwide management program, the major tuna species will in the relatively near future probably be exploited at levels beyond the maximum average sustainable yields. This will be to the disadvantage of all nations. However, a worldwide management agency that can appropriately take into account the various objectives of all nations cannot be achieved quickly.

Any economic zone alternative without rational high seas tuna management regulation will not prevent excess fishing effort and the associated biological and economic waste. Also, because of the flexibility and mobility of the tuna fleets, area by area or species by species management plans cannot be effective over time. Certainly piecemeal regulations by regional (even oceanwide) commissions acting independently will not bring about desirable results.

Therefore, considering the importance of timely decisions relative to tuna management, it may be more realistic to consider the establishment of a management scheme that includes certain aspects of the three arrangements described in this paper—economic zones, regional commissions, and a global organization.

For example, it should be possible to establish a global tuna council. Representation on the council could include tuna fishing states, coastal states from areas where tuna occur, and possibly non–tuna fishing states. Acceptable representation would have to be determined by the world community, but would also have to be acceptable to the states currently involved in tuna fishing. This council could then establish certain criteria or guidelines which would be used as a management framework within which each regional commission would operate. The council could serve as a coordinating agency among the commissions for research and statistics collection. It could also set out general procedures to be followed in establishing regulatory techniques such as national quotas and license fees and for enforcement of regulations.

The regional commission might, however, be responsible for establishing specific catch quotas and for assuring that national quotas, if used, apply within the jurisdiction of the coastal states as well as on the high seas. The commission could see that license fees are consistent among coastal states and that the fees also apply to catches on the high seas.

The commission, working with the coastal states, could be responsible for enforcement. This would require close working relations between the coastal states and the commission in each ocean.

Certain specific questions, such as whether the fishermen of a coastal state should be required to pay a license fee for fishing within the waters of the coastal state, would have to be answered. It would seem that for the system to be effective, license fees, if charged for anyone, should apply to everyone. Perhaps the fees paid by the fishermen of a given coastal state could be allocated to that coastal state.

In general, to assure that costs are borne by the users, fees should be allocated jointly to the council, the commissions, and the coastal states.

It seems likely that an approach combining regulated-access economic zones operating under management plans developed by regional commissions, which in turn would be coordinated and guided by general criteria set out by a global tuna council, could, with proper international agreements and cooperation, effectively accomplish all five of the basic objectives of effective tuna management.

References

Anderson, A. W., *et al.* 1953. Survey of the domestic tuna industry. U.S. Fish and Wildlife Service Special Scientific Report —Fisheries No. 104, 436p.

Asada, Y. 1972. Management and investment in Japan's tuna longline fishery. In *Economic Aspects of Fish Production*. Organisation for Economic Cooperation and Development, Paris, pp. 309–318.

Asada, Y. 1973. License limitation regulations: The Japanese system, Food and Agriculture Organization—Fisheries Industry FMD/73/5–23, 18p.

Bell, F. W. 1969. Forecasting world demand for tuna to the year 1990. *Commercial Fisheries Review* 31(12): 24–31.

Blackburn, M. 1965. Oceanography and the ecology of tunas. *Oceanography and Marine Biology Annual Review* 3: 299–322.

Blackburn, M., and R. M. Laurs. 1972. Distribution of forage of skipjack tuna (*Euthynnus pelamis*) in the eastern tropical Pacific. National Oceanic and Atmospheric Administration Technical Report NMFS, SSRF–649, 16p.

Broadhead, G. C. 1971. International trade—tuna. Indian Ocean Fishery Commission, Development Programme, Document 14, 27p.

Brock, V. E. 1959. The tuna resources in relation to oceanographic features. U.S. Fish and Wildlife Service Circular 65: 1–11.

Broderick, D. G. 1973. An industry study: The tuna fishery. Ph.D. Dissertation, Columbia University.

Christy, Francis T., Jr. 1973. *Alternative Arrangements for Marine Fisheries: An Overview*. Resources for the Future, Inc., Washington, D.C.

Clemens, H. B., and G. A. Flittner. 1969. Bluefin tuna migrate across the Pacific Ocean. *California Fish and Game* 55(2): 132–135.

Dwivedi, S. N. 1972. Tuna and oceanographic research. *Mahesgar* 5(2): 80–84.

FAO. 1963. World scientific meeting on the biology of tuna and related species. La Jolla, Calif., Food and Agriculture Organization Fisheries Reports No. 6 (4 vols.).

FAO. 1968. Report of the meeting of a group of experts on tuna stocks. FAO Fisheries Reports No. 61, 45p.

57

FAO. 1971a. Report of the joint meeting of the Indo-Pacific Fisheries
Council . . . and the Indian Ocean Fishery Commission . . . FAO
Fisheries Reports No. 104.

FAO. 1971b. *Yearbook of Fishery Statistics for 1970*. Vol. 30. Rome.

FAO/IOFC/IPFC. 1972. Report of the Meeting of the IOFC/
IPFC *Ad Hoc* Working Party of Scientists Stock Assessment
of Tuna. Rome, June 7–9, 1972. Indian Ocean Fishery Com-
mission/Indo-Pacific Fisheries Council: TM/72/4.

Felando, A. 1972. Statement: Local impacts of the law of the sea.
October 10–12, 1972. Seattle, Washington. 32p.

Fullenbaum, R. E. 1970. A survey of maximum sustainable yield
estimates on a world basis for selected fisheries. Bureau of
Commercial Fisheries, Division of Economic Research, Working Paper No. 43, 78p.

Gulland, J. A. (ed.). 1970. The fish resources of the oceans. FAO
Technical Paper 97, 425p.

Gulland, J. A. 1972. Some thoughts on a global approach to tuna
management. In *Economic Aspects of Fish Production*.
Organisation for Economic Cooperation and Development, Paris,
pp. 228–238.

Hayasi, S. 1972. Biological views for conservation of yellowfin
tuna in the Atlantic Ocean, based on information obtained up to
October 1972. International Commission for the Conservation
of Atlantic Tunas/SCRS No. 21.

Hela, I., and T. Laevastu. 1970. *Fisheries Hydrography*. Fishing
News (Books) Ltd., London.

Hester, F. J., and T. Otsu. 1973. A review of the literature on
the development of skipjack tuna fisheries in the central and
western Pacific Ocean. National Oceanic and Atmospheric
Administration Technical Report NMFS, SSRF–661, 13p.

ICCAT. 1971. Proceedings of the Second Regular Meeting of the
Commission.

Japanese Tuna Fisheries Federation. 1969. Statistics of Japanese
Tuna Fishery. Tokyo.

Joseph, J. 1970. Management of tropical tunas in the eastern
Pacific Ocean. *Transactions of the American Fisheries Society*
99(3): 629–648.

Joseph, J. 1972. An overview of the tuna fisheries of the world. In
Economic Aspects of Fish Production. Organisation for Economic
Cooperation and Development, Paris, pp. 203–219.

Joseph, J. 1973. The scientific management of the world stocks of
tunas, billfishes and related species. FAO–FI–FMD/73/S–48,
23p.

Kikawa, S., T. Koto, C. Shingu, and Y. Nishikawa. 1969. Status of tuna fisheries in the Indian Ocean as of 1968. Far Seas Fisheries Research Laboratory, S Series 2, 28p.

Laevastu, T., and H. Rosa, Jr. 1963. Distribution and relative abundance of tunas in relation to their environment. In FAO Fisheries Reports No. 6, Vol. 3, pp. 1835–1851.

Mather, F. J., III, and M. R. Bartlett. 1962. Bluefin tuna concentration found during a longline exploration of the northwestern Atlantic slope. *Commercial Fisheries Review* 24(2):1–7.

Moal, R. A. 1972. Cooperation in tropical tuna fishing—Economic aspects of fish production. In *Economic Aspects of Fish Production*. Organisation for Economic Cooperation and Development, Paris, pp. 239–256.

Nakamura, H. 1969. *Tuna Distribution and Migration*. Fishing News (Books) Ltd., London, 76p.

Orange, C. 1961. Spawning of yellowfin tuna and skipjack in the eastern tropical Pacific, as inferred from studies of gonad development. *Inter-American Tropical Tuna Commission Bulletin* 5: 459–526.

Pearcy, W. G. 1971. Remote sensing and the pelagic fisheries environment off Oregon. Proc. of the Symposium on Remote Sensing in Marine Biology and Fishery Resources. Texas A&M University, SG–71–106:158–171.

Rothschild, B. J. 1972. An exposition on the definition of fishing effort. In *Economic Aspects of Fish Production*. Organisation for Economic Cooperation and Development, Paris, pp. 257–271.

Sakagawa, G. T., and W. H. Lenarz. 1972. American participation in tuna fishery of eastern tropical Atlantic. *Marine Fisheries Review* 34(11–12):55–65.

Scientific Committee on Resource Sampling. 1972. Report of the meeting of the special working group on stock assessment of yellowfin tuna. No. 7 Abidjan, June 12–16, 1972.

Shomura, R. S. 1966. The Atlantic tuna fisheries, 1963. *Commercial Fisheries Review* 28(5):1–11.

U.S. Department of Commerce. 1973. *Fisheries of the United States, 1972*. U.S. Government Printing Office, Washington, D.C., p. 53.

Yabe, H., Y. Yabuta, and S. Ueyanagi. 1963. Comparative distribution of eggs, larvae and adults in relation to biotic and abiotic environmental factors. In FAO Fisheries Reports No. 6, Vol. 3, pp. 979–1009.

Resources for the Future
Program of International Studies of Fishery Arrangements
Paper Series

Paper, $3.00 each
(except as noted)